Cover Copy

Secrets can be titillating...
Secrets can be dangerous...
Will Rosamonde's secrets kill her, or save her?

Lady Rosamonde Raven was a girl of seventeen when the Earl of Winterly rescued her from tragic death. Six years later, he arrives at her father's country estate for a house party and she is still irresistibly attracted to him. Unfortunately, her father has agreed to a betrothal between her and an arrogant marquess who is more than twice her age. She is shocked at her father's decision, but even more so, she's shocked to learn exactly how evil the marquess truly is. There is only one man she trusts with disclosing the truth—Winterly.

There is only one woman Winterly is now set on—Rosamonde. When his lady entrusts the truth of her betrothal with him, he devises a plan. A secret marriage. He simply can't step away from her during her greatest time of need, only when she is kidnapped by the marquess, he must ride out and save her a second time. Flying into a storm of danger, dark secrets, and deadly assignations, he enters a veritable house of terror.

Can he find and rescue his lady before he loses her forever? Or is he already too late?

Books by Joanne Wadsworth

The Matheson Brothers Series
Highlander's Desire, Book One
Highlander's Passion, Book Two
Highlander's Seduction, Book Three
Highlander's Kiss, Book Four
Highlander's Heart, Book Five
Highlander's Sword, Book Six
Highlander's Bride, Book Seven
Highlander's Caress, Book Eight
Highlander's Touch, Book Nine
Highlander's Shifter, Book Ten
Highlander's Claim, Book Eleven
Highlander's Courage, Book Twelve
Highlander's Mermaid, Book Thirteen

Highlander Heat Series
Highlander's Castle, Book One
Highlander's Magic, Book Two
Highlander's Charm, Book Three
Highlander's Guardian, Book Four
Highlander's Faerie, Book Five
Highlander's Champion, Book Six
Highlander's Captive (Short Story)

Billionaire Bodyguards Series
Billionaire Bodyguard Attraction, Book One
Billionaire Bodyguard Boss, Book Two
Billionaire Bodyguard Fling, Book Three

Books by Joanne Wadsworth

Regency Brides Series
The Duke's Bride, Book One
The Earl's Bride, Book Two
The Wartime Bride, Book Three
The Earl's Secret Bride, Book Four
The Prince's Bride, Book Five
Her Pirate Prince, Book Six
Chased by the Corsair, Book Seven

Princesses of Myth Series
Protector, Book One
Warrior, Book Two
Hunter (Short Story - Included in Warrior, Book Two)
Enchanter, Book Three
Healer, Book Four
Chaser, Book Five
Pirate Princess, Book Six

The Earl's

Secret Bride

Regency Brides, Book Four

JOANNE WADSWORTH

The Earl's Secret Bride
ISBN-13: 978-1-98301-324-9
Copyright © 2018, Joanne Wadsworth
Cover Art by Joanne Wadsworth
First electronic publication: June 2018

Joanne Wadsworth
http://www.joannewadsworth.com

AUTHOR'S NOTE:
This book is a work of fiction. The names, characters, places, and incidents are products of the writer's imagination or have been used fictitiously and are not to be construed as real. Any resemblance to persons, living or dead, actual events, locale or organizations is entirely coincidental. The author does not have any control over and does not assume any responsibility for third-party websites or their content.

Published in the United States of America

First digital publication: June 2018
First print publication: June 2018

A Tragic Night Never Forgotten

Along the forest road through Bampton Grange, Cumbria, England, 1805.

Lady Rosamonde Raven stuck her nose against the window as she and her mother, the Countess of Hillhurst, traveled the darkened forest road to London, her breath fogging the glass. Twisting layers of mist swirled a murky yellow-gray from the lamp atop their carriage. She'd traveled this road to town from their country estate dozens of times and it wasn't unusual for the mist to be this thick so close to the change in seasons. Soon winter would be fully upon them and travel made far more difficult. She'd be in London by then though, attending her first Season as a debutante. Bouncing on her seat, she couldn't refrain from allowing her excitement its release.

"Rosamonde, please cease jiggling about and sit back like a lady ought to." Mother's words should have sounded abrupt, but they were laced with love, a smile in her eyes.

"Put your gloves back on and fold your hands in your lap, my dear child. The tips of your fingers are turning blue, the same as your nose now is since being pressed against the window. I don't want you catching a chill. It would ruin your first ball in a week's time if you were sneezing on every gentleman who asked you to dance."

"Yes, Mother." Smiling, she eased back into the plush blue squabs and tugged her dainty white gloves on. Their carriage wasn't cold, not when they'd only recently stopped at the last inn along the route for a meal, their coachman having added hot coals to the brazier which emitted a lovely heat near her slippered feet. "Tell me all about your first Season. Did you dance with Father at your debut ball?"

"I did." Mother pressed a gentle hand over her chest. "He appeared so dashing and handsome and I was already in love with him by then. We'd known each other during our childhood, of course. I enjoyed quite a bit of freedom that night compared to so many of the young ladies debuting."

"What do you mean by freedom?"

"During the first week of my debut, my parents hadn't yet traveled down from the country. I'd been staying with Flora and her family in her parents' townhouse. Flora has always been one of my dearest friends, her mother chaperoning us both. Seventeen, I'd been at the time, only a month shy of turning eighteen."

"I can't imagine attending my debut ball without you."

"I will be there every step of the way." Mother squeezed her hand, her gaze turning thoughtful as she glanced out the window, old memories clearly stirring.

"During my first ball, my parents had already made it quite clear that they wished for me to wed a titled gentleman, that I wouldn't be permitted to marry the third son of an earl, which your father was."

"This is before Father's two elder brothers passed away?"

"Yes, and in order to discourage my infatuation with your father, my father had swiftly entered into negotiations with a gentleman he deemed acceptable for me to marry."

"Who was that gentleman?" As a child, her mother had told her the story about how her father had spirited her away to Gretna Green so they might wed, which she'd thought incredibly romantic upon hearing.

"His name shall always remain a secret." Mother crossed her heart. "Your father bade me to never speak of his name and I have always abided by his decision. I simply knew I couldn't marry any other man, other than your father, so when he was unable to procure a blessing from my parents, he rode for the townhouse where I was staying and stole inside. He kidnapped me, although I was rather willing to be kidnapped, and together we traveled by carriage for nigh on five days so we might reach the Scottish border before my parents heard of what had happened.

"But your parents eventually forgave Father for kidnapping you, didn't they?"

"Yes, but only following the deaths of your two uncles, once your father had become the Earl of Hillhurst." Mother lifted her gaze to the ceiling and blew a kiss toward the heavens. "May your uncles forever rest in peace."

"I wish I could've met both my uncles and my

maternal and paternal grandparents. Why must death come so soon to those we love?"

"There is no rhyme or reason. It is simply the way of life, my dear. No one knows when their time will end on this Earth, which is why we must take every day given to us and embrace it." Leaning forward, Mother kissed her brow. "My child, let us speak of happier times now. Are you eager to see Lady Olivia, Flora's daughter?"

"Incredibly eager." Her mother's dearest friend, Flora, had become Lady Winterly after her marriage to an earl, and Flora's daughter, Olivia, had become her best friend in the years since. "It has been so incredibly long since Olivia and her mother both last stayed with us. Olivia spoke in her last letter of visiting Madam Gonnier's shop in town and having a dozen beautiful new gowns made for the Season. May we visit the same dressmaker too?"

"What a wonderful idea. Of course we may." Her mother cupped her cheek. "Your father has given me complete freedom with your wardrobe for this coming Season while we're in town. He will join us as soon as his negotiations with the Marquess of Roth are all in order."

"I wish..." She released a long sigh, unable to finish what she wanted to say. It was best not to go against Father's wishes regarding his decision to unite their family with the Marquess of Roth's by way of her marriage to the older gentleman. She understood why she would soon be betrothed to the marquess whose property abutted theirs. Father had explained that he intended to ensure she continued living comfortably and that their family's social position remained strong. He also wished to be on better terms with their neighbor following a disagreement that had spanned over thirty years. She'd asked her father what disagreement that had been, only he hadn't wished to delve into it. Let bygones be bygones, he'd said. Deep in her heart though, she'd always hoped to marry for love since her own parents had, not to wed a man who had already buried two wives and five children. Goodness, but the marquess was the same age as her father, which made her shudder. Unfortunately, that was often the way with marriages within the *ton*, particularly when a titled gentleman required a young wife to bear him an heir. She only hoped she might be able to enjoy at least one Season before her father announced her coming betrothal to Lord Roth. She longed to be able to enjoy her debut, being able to see the glitter and experience the thrill of the balls to come, the sparkling gowns worn by the ladies, the jewels adorning their necks, and the chance to dance with Olivia's brother who had become the new Earl of Winterly following the sad passing of Olivia's papa several months ago. She'd always had a secret attraction to Olivia's brother. Winterly and her brother, Avery, had formed a strong friendship.

"What it is you wish for, my dear?" Mother quirked a brow, the pretty blue feathers atop her hat fluttering. "You've got the strangest look on your face."

"It's nothing."

"No, you must tell me."

"Well, Lord Roth can be so stern." She bit into her bottom lip. "He's always grumping and growling, as if he can't find anything to be happy about."

"I agree, but perhaps all he needs is a lady's gentle touch to remedy that sternness. He has suffered a great deal of loss over the years."

"Speaking of that loss. His late wives hardly ever left Rothgale Manor. I certainly never saw them in the nearby village or at any local gathering. I fear that even though Roth lives on our neighboring property, that I might never get to see you as often as I'd like."

"He has promised your father that you will be permitted to visit us, as often as you wish."

"Why is he so interested in me? Roth could take his pick from any of the unwed ladies of the *ton*?"

"That is true, but well, the two women he wed gave him only daughters, of which none survived beyond three years of age. I gave your father four sons before I birthed you and Roth believes that you would follow in my suit by giving him plenty of sons." Mother took a deep breath and let it slowly out again. "You would wish for naught and hold the title of the Marchioness of Roth. You'll have all the wealth you desire at your fingertips."

"Yes, of course." She released a heavy sigh. Wealth meant very little if one didn't have happiness too. Yet neither of her parents seemed willing to change their minds on the issue of who she'd wed, and she'd been taught that she must respect her parents' decisions, that she place her family's welfare and interests above her own. Her marriage would certainly aid in dispelling the long-standing disagreement between their families, whatever that disagreement happened to be. It was a shame her father wouldn't speak of it. Doing so might give her more clarity.

"Rosamonde, don't forget that your father is the one who has the final say on your impending betrothal, and his decision is currently made." Mother squeezed her hand.

"An alliance will be sought with Lord Roth, unless of course you hold affection for another gentleman. If there is another, then speak now so we are aware."

"There is no other." Being smitten with a man like Winterly who'd never thought of her as anything other than Avery's little sister didn't count. Winterly was also eight years her senior and wasn't on the lookout for a wife, not when he was still settling into his new duties as the Earl of Winterly. It could be years before he even entered the marriage mart in search of a wife. Hot tears pricked behind her eyes, and not wanting to distress her mother any further, she cast her gaze out the night-shrouded window. At least before she became a wife and a mother herself, she would enjoy time with Olivia and partaking of all her first Season could—

The carriage swerved and she bounced off her seat and smacked into the door.

"Rosamonde, are you all right?" Mother pulled her into her arms, resettled her on the squabs and ran her hands over her. "Do you hurt anywhere?"

"My head." She touched the back of her head and came away with wet fingers. Blood coated them.

"Turn around so I might see the injury." She gave Mother her back and she dabbed the spot with a handkerchief. "It is a small cut, thankfully. Nothing too major. Remain still while I apply some pressure. Hopefully that's all that will be needed to cease the flow of blood."

"Yes, Mother." She held perfectly still as the carriage bumped along the road again, Mother's hand firm upon the back of her head. "What do you think that swerve was all about?" she asked.

"Hmm, perhaps the driver needed to divert a fallen branch or such along the road. All must be well since we're moving along again."

Thump.

She lifted her gaze to the ceiling, the same as Mother did.

Thump, thump, thump.

The coach slowed, decreasing speed, the trees either side of their carriage becoming less of a blur as they came to a complete stop.

"I wonder if we lost a valise during that swerve?" Frowning, Mother peered out the window. "There is no other reason for the coachman to halt."

The horses whinnied and the harnesses jangled.

"Smithy, Jonesy?" Mother called to the driver and the footman up top. "Please inform us of what is going on, and be quick about it." No answer. Mother's frown deepened. "Hold this handkerchief, Rosamonde. I'll take a look outside."

"Perhaps they've both gone back along the road to retrieve the fallen luggage?" She slid her fingers under her mother's fingers on her head and held the cloth in place, while Mother opened the door and poked her head out.

"Yes, that could be what they've done. Such a thing has happened before, although someone always remains with the coach. I don't see them." The hoot of an owl echoed through the trees and Mother plopped back onto the seat. Wrapping her white lacy shawl tighter around her shoulders, Mother eyed her. "We'll give the men a minute or two and if they haven't returned, we shall go outside and find them."

"Let me take a look too." Her mother wasn't wearing her eyeglasses and her eyesight wasn't the best for seeing into the distance without them. She swung her hand from the back of her head and since only a few drops of blood coated the cloth, she handed it back to her mother and clutching her skirts, hopped down onto the gravelly dirt road.

"Rosamonde, stay within my sight." Mother was on her feet again, grasping the doorway.

"It's so hard to see much of anything with this heavy mist." The thick fog drifted all about, along with the stagnant stench of muddy water from the ditch alongside the road. Nighttime insects buzzed about the lamp atop their carriage, the seat where their driver and footman should be, completely vacant. She shivered as the horses rattled their harnesses, their reins not secured but flapping loose down the side of the coach. She crept to the rear where the trunks were stowed on the back—none appeared missing. Cupping her hands to her mouth, she shouted, "Smithy, Jonesy!"

No answer echoed back through the gloomy soup.

Again she yelled their names, and still no answer.

"We'll need to go and look for them. There is no other choice. I've got your cloak." Mother stepped down onto the road beside her with her cloak and swept the warm woolen garment over her shoulders. "We'll stay close together."

The thunderous rumble of hooves shook the ground and she clutched Mother's hand as out of the misty darkness three enormous men in black coats, their faces covered with heavy black fabric with only slits for their eyes, pulled their horses up before them.

"Back into the coach now." Mother shoved her toward the door then snapped a look at the highwaymen. "What have you done to our servants?"

"They won't be returnin', milady." The man who spoke peeled his head covering away and eyed Rosamonde up and down. "Well, well, what have we here? Ye be a pretty wee thing."

"Leave my daughter alone." Mother rushed forward and the rider's horse heaved back on its hind legs. Mother screamed as the horse came down on top of her.

Rosamonde stood in shock as her mother hit the ground, the beast's hooves trampling and crushing her mother's legs. Blood spurted, spraying out in a wide arc, coating Rosamonde's skirts. The brigand laughed as he dismounted. He tossed his reins to one of the other men, pushed her inside the coach and slammed the door shut.

The carriage rocked as the brigand heaved himself into the coachman's seat atop her father's carriage. She grasped the window and flung it open as he shouted to his fellow thugs, "Dump the lady's body where it won't be found. Her daughter should fetch us a pretty penny, either for reward or on one of the vessels in port. I know a rich captain who'd pay to have her as his personal slave on his ship."

Rosamonde screamed and screamed and screamed.

She got flung about as the coach sped down the road.

Another shout and she heaved to the window.

"I said halt," a man atop a horse bellowed as he galloped in beside them. Not one of the highwaymen. He wore fine clothing, his blue greatcoat lined in fur and flapping over his stallion's rump, a pistol in one of his hands as he aimed it at the driver. Olivia's brother. The

Earl of Winterly was here? She blinked a few times, but he wasn't an illusion, and she'd never mistake Winterly, not when she'd spent such a great deal of time in his company whenever he visited Hillhurst Hall to see Avery. Winterly glanced once at her, then aimed at the highwayman and—*boom*.

The brigand toppled and crashed to the ground with a sickening crunch, the back wheels of the coach running right over him.

Winterly spurred his horse on faster, caught the flying reins and slowed the coach until it rocked to a stop.

She scrambled out the door and fell into his arms. "Oh, Winterly, please, my mother is back on the road. There are two other highwaymen."

"They're already dead, Rosamonde. I was out tonight traveling with my brother who's home on leave, as well as the Duke of Ashten. We dispatched the outlaws rather quickly and my brother is taking care of the countess. Ashten rides to the nearest village and will bring the doctor." He swung her onto his stallion then hoisted up behind her. With his arms wrapped around her, his reins once more in hand, he thrust his knees into his horse's flanks and they bolted forward into the misty gloom. "Are you all right?" he asked in her ear.

"I n-need t-to—" She shivered from head to toe, her lips icy-cold.

"You'll be safe with me. I give you my word, you will."

"I've always been safe with you." She snuggled deeper into his hold, the cloying mist swirling and parting as they galloped through it. Winterly's muscular legs pinned hers against his horse, his legs encased in dark riding breeches, his body emitting immense warmth and solid strength. "I can't lose my mother, Winterly."

"You're not going to, not if I have any say in the matter." A gruff growl.

"Please, hurry." The wind whipped past, the flimsy skirts of her light-blue muslin day gown flapping. She shivered violently.

Winterly curled one arm around her waist and tucked her even tighter against him, his lips pinched into a tight white line. "What did you witness in regard to the attack?"

"Everything, although Mother tried to push me away."

"I'm sorry, so sorry." Finally he slowed his mount.

Up ahead, his brother, Harry, sat in his regimental uniform on the side of the road cradling her mother in his arms, her eyes shut and face deathly pale. The bodies of the other two highwaymen were lumped in the ditch.

"Lady Rosamonde is with me and has come to no harm." Winterly pulled his snorting stallion to a halt, bounded down and gripped her waist. He settled her on her feet beside her mother.

Immense grief and pain tore through her as she dropped to her knees. Hot tears burned behind her eyes and cascaded free as she cupped Mother's cold cheeks. "You will survive, Mother. Do not give up the fight. I need you. Father needs you. My brothers need you. We won't survive without you."

"She'll survive." Winterly hunkered down beside her, the striking color of his blue eyes filled with firm assurance. He tucked her closer into his side, her mother's ragged breathing all that broke the silence.

Chapter 1

Hillhurst Hall, Penrith, England, near the Scottish Borders, six years later, 1811.

"This is such a heinous subject matter, Mother." Rocking in the chair at her mother's bedside, Rosamonde arched a brow over the thick pages of the volume she'd collected from Hillhurst Hall's library this morning. "Are you absolutely certain you wish for me to read this particular book?"

"Yes, that's the one I wish for you to read." Fluffing her lace-edged white pillow, Mother nestled back more comfortably in her bed, her pink and yellow floral bedcovers folded neatly at her waist and a waiting look on her face. "Indeed it is. Do begin, my dear child."

"I'll begin after you tell me why you have a sudden wish to read about ghostly wanderers?" She tapped the title emblazoned on the front of the black leather-bound cover. *Peculiar Warnings Volume Two, The Ghostly Wanderer of the Moors.*

"Well, you see, Lady Winterly sent me the book and if I haven't read at least the first chapter of it before she and her daughter arrive for our house party tomorrow then she will be sorely disappointed."

"I wasn't aware Lady Winterly had a love of such, ah, scandalous novels. She should have sent a book of poems or even a fanciful romance as she usually does, not a novel of abject horror." She would have a word with Lady Winterly when she arrived, except the lady she considered a second mother would likely do naught but smile and hug her instead of taking any warning truly to heart.

"Perhaps Flora wishes for me to read something different for a change." A wrinkle of Mother's nose. "This may be my fault. I mentioned to Flora in my last letter that I find some days rather difficult and tedious, being that I can't travel as easily with these useless legs of mine. The book arrived soon after with a note saying, 'Here is something different for a change.'"

"If you wish to travel to London, to either call on your friends, attend the opera, enjoy a ride through the park, or visit a museum or two, then you need only say. Father is riding to town next month and we can travel with him." Neither of them had traveled much since that dreadful night six years ago. She'd been her mother's constant companion ever since, a task she both adored and took quite seriously.

"No, I'd much rather stay right here in the country with you." Mother shook her head, her words slightly jittery.

She let the topic go since it was clearly causing her mother some distress and instead lifted the book and turned to the first page. Sending her rocking chair into a gentle rock with the push of one foot, she tucked one lock of errant hair behind her ear and eyed the first chapter. "Then allow me to begin."

"Chapter One. The shadowed dawn of the new day brought the Highland mist swirling with icy tendrils across the craggy moors. Count Colbert dug his shovel deep into the stony ground and tipped the mound of gritty soil onto the rubbly pile beside him. Six feet deep was the requirement for this hole, as requested by his father, the recently deceased Count Clement. His father had chosen this remote spot on the barren hillside overlooking the Scottish Borders as where he wished his final resting place to be, information his son had recovered from his father's private papers. Once again, he plunged his shovel into the ground and heaved. When the burial plot met with his requirements, he wiped his dirtied hands on the sides of his finely tailored breeches, slowly stepped around his father's body wrapped in the library mat and bowing his head respectfully, issued a quick prayer, then heaved."

Shuddering, Rosamonde slammed the book shut and dropped it into her lap, the black leather of the volume a stark contrast of color to the white skirts of her day gown. "I believe that concludes the first chapter, Mother."

"Oh, wonderful. I do detest tediously long chapters." With a smile of gratitude, Mother scooped her embroidery basket from where her lady's maid had left it earlier in the morning on the bedcovers and tugged it closer. With tapestry cloth and needle in hand, Mother frowned. "Oh, I need more red thread. I'm almost out of it. Could you fetch me a spool from the cabinet in your father's study?"

"Of course." She set the novel on the side table, kissed Mother's warm cheek and crossed the spacious chamber decorated in the vivid colors of spring. After the accident, Father had transformed this room on the lower floor of their country estate for Mother, while he'd ordered the adjoining chamber to be made available for himself. The lower floor offered Mother more options. When she wished to move freely about in her wheeled chair, without the need of a footman to carry her up and down the stairs, she very easily could.

Once she'd closed Mother's bedchamber door, she wandered along the lower passageway, her footsteps muffled by the deep red and gold woven hallway runner. Outside Father's study, she poised her hand on the knob but halted as voices drifted to her. Raised voices. Father's and another man's.

Pressing one ear to the paneled wood, she tried to pick whose voice it was.

"I didn't realize you wished for a possible match with my daughter, not when your previous betrothal to her came to an end due to my wife's accident. I thought you understood my daughter is needed here." Clear frustration tinged Father's tone.

"I didn't press for the match following the accident, not when your wife needed her, but I don't believe the countess requires her daughter's full companionship any longer. It's been six years, Hillhurst." A gruff answer, the voice now unmistakable. It belonged to the Marquess of Roth.

The marquess had visited a time or two each year, usually to complain about something or other to Father, disagreements they had relating to their joint land border to the north.

"Instead of marrying your daughter," the marquess muttered, "I wed another lady and with her death from childbirth recently, I am again in a quandary. I require a son, Hillhurst, and you owe me a damned favor, a rather large one at that."

"I might consider a possible betrothal in six months' time. Certainly no sooner."

"That is unacceptable," Roth roared. "Your wife has not only birthed you four healthy sons, but your daughter could do the same for me. If you withhold from me, then I'll withhold from you. I demand repayment of the funds you borrowed from me. The loan I extended to you has now come to an end."

"The loan will be repaid in five years' time, exactly as specified in our agreement."

"Damn it, man. You stole your countess from me."

"Elizabeth was never yours."

"She should have been my wife all those years ago, and you know it," the marquess hissed.

Shock flared through her. Was Lord Roth the titled gentleman her mother's father had hoped to tie her mother to in marriage? If he was, then it was no wonder her parents had never spoken the man's name to her or her brothers in all these years.

"Elizabeth chose me," Father snapped back.

"Elizabeth's father chose me. You, Hillhurst, would not be wed to your wife if you hadn't kidnapped her and snuck her away to Gretna Green." Glass shattered and Roth shouted, "You shall announce my betrothal to Lady Rosamonde immediately, otherwise I shall call in the loan and you'll repay every penny owed to me. If you don't do as I say, you could lose a damned lot. I'll see to it that you do."

Silence. Utter silence.

Rosamonde's heart thumped.

A minute passed. Two minutes.

Finally, her father's voice echoed back to her. "Fine. I will inform my daughter that she is now betrothed to you, and that your marriage will take place in six months."

"I'm not waiting six months before she and I can speak vows. We will wed at the end of this month. You have twenty-eight days in total, not a single day more, Hillhurst."

"Roth, we are expecting house guests this week. My wife and I don't have time to organize a wedding given that kind of short notice."

"You don't need to organize a thing. I shall do it all. I also expect an invitation to attend this house party, so I might spend some time with my soon-to-be wife." A storm of footsteps, and the door swung open. Roth stood there, his gray eyes as cold as the heavy clouds growing even heavier through Father's square-cut study window. Roth glared at her, his nostrils flaring and his chin flapping. "Lady Rosamonde, it appears you like to eavesdrop on conversations. Well, so be it. You should know that your father and I have come to an agreement, that you and I are now betrothed, with our wedding set to take place at the end of the month. As my wife, I expect you to be submissive to my authority, and to bear me as many sons as I so desire. Is that understood?"

Shocked by his audacity, she couldn't utter a word.

"Good. No words of opposition. That is a welcome start to our future nuptials." He grasped her hand and planted a slobbery kiss across the back of her knuckles. "Following our marriage, you shall be permitted to visit Hillhurst Hall, but only once you're expecting my child and not a day before."

"I, ah."

His fingernails bit into her palm. "I can see you're a little overwhelmed by the news of our betrothal. I shall return—let's see, not tomorrow, but the day after. Have one of your footmen bring a picnic basket down to the lake. I'll meet you there at midday. We can enjoy some time together."

"My lord, I—"

"There is no need to give me your thanks." With a tug on his severely knotted black cravat, he heaved past her and marched down the passageway, his cane tapping the floor and the scent of pipe-smoke clinging to his morning coat, drifting back to her.

"Come in, Rosamonde, and close the door behind you." Father released a long sigh as he sank back into his forest-green leather chair behind his polished oak desk.

"Open the blasted door, you idiot!"

She jumped as Roth yelled at their butler, then the front door clicked open and clicked shut after the marquess as he left. Her stomach knotted into an awful mess as she closed Father's study door. "He is so rude, dismissive, and curt."

"More so than ever before, I'm afraid." Father motioned to the forest-green settee next to the oak side table holding a decanter and glasses, the glittering spread of fine crystal on the floor under the window the clear remnants of another glass. "Take a seat, my child."

Primly, she sat, adjusting the gold-patterned cushion at her back before crossing her ankles and facing her father. The gray streaks either side of her father's dark head were combed perfectly back, blending into the dark brown. "Please, Father, tell me I do not have to wed Roth."

"I wasn't aware you were outside the door." He dropped his head back against the high headrest of his chair.

"I'm sorry. I didn't mean to eavesdrop on your conversation, but Mother needed some red thread and I was about to knock when I heard yours and the marquess's raised voices."

"Exactly what did you hear?"

"That there is a debt owed, that you stole Mother from him. Is he the titled gentleman that mother's father wished for her to wed?"

"Yes, and I'm sorry you had to hear all that you did."

"Mother still needs me."

"Yes, I understand that, but Roth has demanded repayment of the loan if I don't agree to your betrothal, which as you heard, I have now done. You are to wed him at the end of the month." Turning his troubled gaze to the window overlooking the front drive, Father watched Roth stepping into his carriage. The driver snapped the reins and Roth's horses moved into a swift trot, his carriage disappearing down their drive lined with fastidiously trimmed topiary trees. "Roth is rather determined in his quest for an heir, which I understand since he is a marquess."

"He has no brothers, correct?"

"None to speak of, although he'll have other male relatives somewhere within his paternal line. I dare say he is also a stubborn man and you shall need to assert yourself once you're wed to him." Heavy, conceding words as Father leaned forward and pressed his elbows to the desktop, the leather of his chair creaking. "Rosamonde, you are three and twenty and must soon wed. I would also like to point out the benefits of marrying Roth. He is our neighbor and has already said he'd never halt you from visiting your mother. There is that to consider."

"Only once I'm with child." She rolled her eyes. "I detest him. He is a wretched man. Did you ever get the chance to meet any of his first three wives?" She certainly never had, not even his third wife whom Roth had wed only one month following her mother's accident.

"Yes, your mother and I paid a call to Rothgale Manor, only once though, ten years after I swept your mother away to Gretna Green. We met his second wife at the time, but we never did meet his first wife or the third unfortunately. The ladies always preferred keeping to themselves." At her quick intake of breath, Father raised a staying hand. "I understand that's strange that they preferred doing so, but they simply did. Regarding the loan though, it is quite substantial, and if not for Roth offering to lend me the money when he did, then I would have been forced to sell our townhouse and all our unentailed land which I've worked hard to acquire. I now have several investments on the go, but none I'm able to cash in soon. I must wait for the profits from those investments to become available, which will be five years from now. Spend some time with him, my child. Be welcoming."

"That's your advice?"

"For your mother's sake, yes. She isn't aware of the loan, and neither is Avery. She would be in great despair if she ever learnt Roth had brought up her past in persuading me to agree to his forthcoming marriage to you. Both her and Avery must think that you have no issue marrying the man, that you desire a secure future as his marchioness. Do you think you can be convincing?"

"So I have no other choice?" She would do anything for her mother, her brothers, and her father too. She pinched the bridge of her nose, an ache forming behind her eyes.

"Yes, there is no other choice."

"Father—"

"I'm sorry, Rosamonde." His apology was spoken firmly but gently. "Surely you didn't expect to remain unmarried forever?"

"No, but I had hoped to form a certain attachment to the gentleman I wished to wed, or whom you chose for me. You and Mother love each other."

"Marriages within Society are made for many reasons, although unfortunately most of them have very little to do with love. Your marriage would benefit our family greatly, but if there is a man you wish for me to consider as your future husband, then you must speak up now. This is your last chance."

Images of Winterly fluttered through her mind, of how

he'd rescued her from those brigands six years ago, of how he'd kept her safe from harm, of how she'd always been rather smitten with him, and of how he'd been the only man to ever stir her heart. Not that Winterly had ever shown any interest in her, other than for being her friend. Bowing her head, she nodded her acquiescence. "Announce the betrothal. I shall convince Mother and Avery that I wish to wed the marquess."

"Thank you, my child. I shall send Roth my written confirmation of your betrothal, as well as requesting his word that he will no longer demand repayment of the loan until such time as it is actually due." He removed a piece of paper from his top drawer, dipped his quill into his ink bottle and wrote.

She opened her mouth, then closed it again, swallowing any further protest she might have considered. Outside, a jagged spike of lightning slashed the dreary morning skies. Rain pinged off the window and drenched the gravel drive and the front lawn. She rose from her chair and gripped the forest-green painted windowsill. For her family's sake, she must consign herself to this coming marriage. No other choice remained.

"I see Roth has just visited, Father, and thankfully left." Avery strode into the room, cutting a suave figure in his fine black jacket and tan breeches. He halted as he took one look at her, then father, then her again. He closed the door, a frown marring his brow as he tugged on the hem of his tan waistcoat. "My apologies if I've interrupted an important conversation between the two of you. Rosamonde, are you all right? You look sad."

"I'm fine, Avery." She forced a smile to her face.

"No apology needed, my son." Father cleared his throat, then gestured to her, a dot of ink splattering the paper. "I would have sought you out soon myself. Lord Roth shall be joining us for our house party. He and Rosamonde are now betrothed. Do wish your sister well on her upcoming nuptials."

"Pardon?" Her brother's face paled. "Is this true?" he demanded as he swung a look at her.

With Avery she'd have to take all care, otherwise he and Mother would learn the truth, and the last thing she wished to do was to worry either of them. She released her gripping hold on the windowsill, her stomach dipping at the lie she would now speak with her brother. With an incline of her head, she murmured, "Yes, please wish me well."

Heaven help her, but she'd have to find a way to make things work with Lord Roth.

Chapter 2

Underneath the powerful hooves of his stallion, the ground shook as Richard Trentbury, the Earl of Winterly, urged his mount along the country road toward Hillhurst Hall. He'd left his country estate at dawn to make the four-hour ride across country, his valet having already gone on ahead yesterday with his mother and sister in their carriage. They'd all be here awaiting his arrival.

Breathing deep, he drew in fresh air and grinned. Spending the coming week with Avery and the Earl of Hillhurst's family would be a treat since it had been some time since his last visit. He hadn't been able to make the earl and countess's annual house party last year.

Cutting the corner at a breakneck speed, he savored the invigorating freedom of being as one with nature atop his horse, of setting aside his duties and relaxing into the events that the coming week would hold. Hillhurst had a large property with a decent number of game to hunt, then there was the lake where he and Avery had fished and swum in as lads.

Up ahead, the winding length of Hillhurst Hall's driveway appeared, along with a rider awaiting him near the cluster of trees at the end. Christopher Raven, Viscount Avery, one of his lifelong friends. Grinning, he came to a shuddering halt next to Avery then lifted his hat and tipped it toward him. "Fancy seeing you out here, old chap."

"Yes, fancy that." A responding grin. "Your family arrived yesterday without issue and your mother and mine are both enjoying tea and a chat whereby neither my father or I can get a word in edgewise. Thus, that is why I'm here at the end of the drive awaiting your arrival."

"What of my sister?"

"Olivia is at the lake with Rosamonde, chaperoning her since—" His friend released a long, staggered breath. "We'll discuss that later. The ladies are enjoying a picnic by the lake. They took fishing poles down with them and since Rosamonde usually throws the pole in the water rather than just the line, it would be best if we could rescue those poles before they join the other hundred or so already gracing the bottom of the lake. Our cook made an array of delicious picnic foods." Lifting his nose to the air, Avery sniffed and let out a rumble of hearty appreciation. "I can already smell the roast beef sandwiches, pickled eggs, and ham and egg pie. Can you?"

"No, but then you always could scent food from a mile away." His friend had a true talent in that regard. During their years they'd attended Eton together, he'd enjoyed the odd holiday here at Hillhurst Hall with Avery's family, little Rosamonde always trekking after him and her four older brothers. In her short skirts and pantaloons, she'd gotten into a dratted amount of trouble, more so than his own sisters ever had at their country estate. "How is Rosamonde, other than still adept at losing fishing poles?"

"She is quite out of her mind." Avery tsked under his breath.

"Whatever do you mean? Has she been climbing trees and getting stuck in them again?" The last time he'd seen her she'd been halfway up a tree along this very drive when he'd ridden in with Avery one warm summer morning. She'd been trying to rescue a wee kitten from the upper branches, something she should never have attempted to do on her own, although something Avery had found immensely amusing as he'd watched his sister struggle within the swaying boughs. Rosamonde had growled at her brother and demanded he come up and fetch her and the kitten, but since Avery had been laughing so hard, Winterly had instead been the one to climb up to save Rosamonde and her scraggly-haired pet. When he'd reached her, he'd been shocked to find her wearing a pair of her brother's old breeches, the waist held up with suspenders, and the hem of the long legs rolled to mid-calf. Such beguiling calves she'd had, her golden locks all disheveled and loose about her face. He'd plucked leaves and twigs from her hair before climbing higher and snatching the kitten from its perilous perch. Then he'd aided her while she'd clambered back down and once they both had their feet on solid ground, he'd given her a sound lashing with his tongue. If she'd fallen she could have broken a leg or an arm, or even worse, lost her life. Trees weren't for ladies to climb, but to sit underneath and enjoy the shade they provided on a hot summer's day. She'd huffed and puffed at him, stating her mind rather clearly before thanking him for rescuing her and Marmalade.

"I'll explain what I mean about Rosamonde while we ride to the lake. Let's race. Keep up if you can." Avery thrust his knees into his horse's flanks and took off like a ball being shot from a cannon. With his knee-length riding boots polished to a high sheen and his green riding jacket tailored to his tall form, his friend tucked his head in closer to his horse's neck, the wind at his back.

Winterly bolted after him and when he caught up, they raced side by side across the fields. Over the rushing wind he yelled, "How is Rosamonde out of her mind? Explain now if you will."

"She and the Marquess of Roth are betrothed, their wedding set for the end of the month, and Rosamonde has decreed that she can't wait for that day to arrive. She will be married in twenty-six days, Winterly." A snarl from Avery.

"Surely you jest?" He almost lost his seat. He hadn't even caught the slightest murmur of gossip regarding a possible betrothal between her and Lord Roth, a man who was old enough to be her father, a man who'd buried three wives and five, no, six children now. His third wife had birthed a stillborn son before she'd passed away from childbirth. "It hasn't even been a year since Roth lost his last wife."

"Six months to be exact, but he is desperate for an heir."

"The man is arrogant and detestable." A growled statement as he jumped over a wooden rail then ducked his head under a low branch before cantering around a copse of trees. He and Avery rode directly toward Hillhurst's private lake which shimmered in the distance. "Roth is a terrible match for your sister."

"When I asked Rosamonde if she had any desire to wed Roth, she said her marriage to the marquess would benefit our family greatly. Something more is afoot though. Six years ago, Father had been in negotiations with Roth regarding a marriage between Rosamonde and the marquess, one which would align our two families but those negotiations came to an abrupt end following Mother's accident. Rosamonde was needed at home, and I never thought Father would ever consider going there again, allowing a match with Roth. I hadn't agreed with it the first time, let alone this time either. I fear I won't even get to see my sister once she's wed, particularly since Roth had a tendency to keep his previous wives sequestered under his roof with very little freedom granted to them."

"I never actually got to meet any of Roth's previous wives. Whenever he came to London, he arrived alone." Of course many marriages within their Society were sought for purposes of social and financial advancement, with many young ladies speaking vows with gentlemen twenty, thirty, or even forty years their senior. The ladies desired a standing position within Society, and the men desired a young wife to provide them with children, particularly an heir and a spare.

"Rosamonde certainly isn't fighting Father's wishes, and Mother seems consigned to what is about to happen. Her only concession to it all is that Rosamonde won't be living far away. Roth has also agreed that Rosamonde may return home for visits as often as she'd like, but only once she is already expecting his child." Avery snapped his teeth together. "Damn it, but I don't want to see my sister wed to such a brutish man. She deserves someone who will honor and respect her kind and loving heart. Perhaps you might have a word with her, Winterly? You are one of the few gentlemen outside of our family who she would actually talk to about this issue. She's always admired and respected you. In fact, she's considered you her personal hero ever since you saved her and my mother."

"I'll talk to her." He couldn't allow Rosamonde to wed the marquess without first speaking to her about her decision and understanding the full reasoning behind it, for there was surely more to it than what he'd so far heard.

They rode on and arrived minutes later at the edge of the lake. He brought his steed to a halt on the grassy embankment, just as Avery did. A quick dismount and he looped his reins around a post where his horse could reach the water's edge for a drink.

Avery secured his horse to the same post before wandering down to the rocky shoreline. His friend removed his black leather gloves and tapping them against his thigh, crouched and scooped a pebble. "Choose a stone," Avery demanded with a challenging arch to his brow. "It's been two years since we last skipped stones here."

"I'm no better at it. I don't have a private lake to practice with as you do." He and Avery had skipped stones here often over the years, his friend relentlessly beating him on the number of skips and the distance he could manage. Still, he selected a stone and closing one eye, judged the right spot on the water he intended to hit. A fling and he sent the stone spinning out. It bounced, once, twice, three times, then sunk below the surface.

"That is a pitiful effort." A snort and grin from Avery. "Come, surely you can do better than that?"

"What is the trick to getting it to bounce farther?" He searched the shoreline for another stone, one smoother and flatter than the first.

"The trick is all in the way one turns their wrist." Avery laughed and sent his own stone spinning out. It skipped across the surface an impressive six times before it disappeared below the water.

"Well done." He clapped then prepared himself for his next throw. He sent his stone flying and managed four skips this time—an improvement. "How many skips can Rosamonde manage?"

"Eight is the highest she's reached. I'm not quite sure how she manages it myself, but if you want some tips then she is the one to ask." His friend motioned toward the trees along the embankment where the sweeping branches of a willow dipped into the water and the faint giggle of two ladies echoed back to them. "Our sisters, I believe, are just around the corner."

"Let's be off then." Stuffing his gloves in his coat pocket, he trekked alongside Avery around the lake until they stepped through a cluster of willows. Dappled afternoon sunshine beamed down on the golden-haired heads of two angels. One angel was of course his beloved sister, Olivia, who today was dressed in a daffodil-yellow walking gown, the other angel being Rosamonde. Sweet Rosamonde's shimmery golden curls tumbled over her shoulders and down her back in a silken veil, while a pale pink bonnet sat upon her head with satin ribbons tied underneath her dainty chin. Her long lashes swept her rosy cheeks, her striking eyes reflecting the stunning blues and greens of the rippling water lapping close to her slippered feet. Her dress was sweetly simple, made of pale pink muslin with short capped sleeves trimmed with white lace, a white silk ribbon tied underneath her breasts, the ends of the ribbon fluttering about her bare arms.

Since leaving her childhood behind, she'd become a beautiful lady, her curves womanly, her hips softy rounded, her waist trim and breasts firm and generous, the upper swells of her bosom showing above the low neckline of her gown. She'd become a woman proper, one whom the gentlemen of the *ton* would be clamoring over to meet. An odd thought really, which had his gut clenching in the most uncomfortable way.

Closing his eyes in the hope that the thrall that had suddenly overcome him would just as quickly vanish, he counted to three then opened his eyes again. Unfortunately, the thrall resumed as if it had never ceased. Her lush lips tipped upward at the corners as she smiled at him, the innocent twinkle in her eyes a painfully arousing reminder that she would soon belong to the Marquess of Roth, a condescending man who didn't deserve such an angelic beauty at his side.

Avery clapped him on the shoulder. "Speak to Rosamonde now if you wish. I'll divert Olivia. See if you can uncover my sister's true thoughts about Roth. I'm relying on you, my friend."

"Of course." He waved to his sister and Olivia waved back, the two of them having only spoken yesterday.

Avery left his side and joined the ladies. His friend

snuck the fishing pole from Rosamonde's hands and motioned toward him with a few words to Rosamonde he couldn't quite catch, although which must be something along the lines of her greeting him since she nodded at her brother and sashayed toward him with a welcoming grin.

"Lord Winterly, it's wonderful to see you've arrived."

"Lady Rosamonde." He removed his hat and dipped his head. "You are a fetching sight and quite stunned me just now."

"I did?" A blush stole across her high cheeks as she lowered into a curtsy, her gaze going to the grass then lifting again as she met his eyes. "That is very nice of you to say. You look quite dashing yourself, as if you've had a rather invigorating ride from your country estate."

"Extremely invigorating. It's been far too long since my last visit."

"Yes, we need to have more house parties, not just a yearly one."

"Or you could travel to town. I'm in London at least six months of the year."

"Mother still won't travel to town, I'm afraid. The most she manages is the local village."

"You're always welcome at my townhouse." He caught her gloved hand and kissed the back of her knuckles. "Olivia would adore having you stay. The fun you two could get up to would keep me on my toes for days."

"Well, I'm not sure I can visit, but I'll endeavor to keep you on your toes while you're here instead."

"Walk with me so we can catch up." He tucked her hand around his bent arm and steered her toward the tartan blanket laid out on the grass underneath one of the trees. "Have you caught any fish yet this morning?"

"No, and I sometimes wonder if there are actually any fish in this lake to catch." She tapped her lower lip, her rather deliciously full lower lip.

"I've heard some interesting news from your brother." It was best he get right to the point. "You're to be married to the Marquess of Roth?"

"Yes." She fumbled in her step and he tightened his hold on her. "Ah, Lord Roth shall be joining us soon. He asked me to organize this picnic by the lake for midday so he might be able to get to know me better."

"Speaking of Roth, perhaps you might explain a few things to me." Keeping his tone low, he leaned in closer, drawing in her sweet fragrance of raspberries and vanilla, a unique scent he'd only ever caught on her. "Why are you marrying him?"

"Did Avery put you up to asking that question?"

"Your brother loves you, has only your best interests at heart."

"I love my brother too."

"You haven't had a Season yet, Rosamonde."

"My mother's good health and welfare comes first."

"I understand that, but Roth's nature doesn't suit your own."

"I wasn't aware that needed to be a prerequisite for marriage." She arched a brow, her chin lifting as she met his gaze. "You know as well as I do that ladies wed for far more important reasons than that."

"Yes, but what exactly is your reason for agreeing to this marriage?"

"Duty to my family."

"Be truthful with me."

"I was." A huff, her lips pouting prettily.

"Then be more truthful." He'd get the answer out of her.

"If I tell you exactly why, then you'll blab to my brother. Your friendship with him overrides any friendship you've ever had with me." Her blue-green eyes held a spirited flare he'd always admired, and they flared with golden sparks right now.

"So there is more to the betrothal than what you've so far alluded to?"

"Of course there is, not that I intend on telling you." She pulled her hand from his arm and marched toward the picnic blanket.

He marched after her. She had such incredible fight, although so did he, and he wasn't leaving until he'd gotten his answer.

Chapter 3

Rosamonde stormed toward the forest-green and white tartan blanket laid out underneath the large willow, her father's footman standing nearby. "Thank you, Heathcoat, but you may return to the house now that my brother and the Earl of Winterly have arrived. Perhaps return in another hour with the dessert basket."

"Yes, my lady." Heathcoat acknowledged her with a short bow then clipped his heels together and strode through the trees toward the rolling fields where Hillhurst Hall rose tall and stately on the hilly rise a half mile distant.

"Are you angry with me?" Winterly caught up to her.

"Yes. And no. It is difficult enough knowing my future path is now decided without having to explain why. I need you to offer your support with my upcoming marriage, just as I need my brother's support."

"I didn't say I wouldn't offer my support, and neither has Avery."

"The insinuation is there since you both clearly

disagree with my decision." She plopped down onto the blanket, rather ungracefully. Winterly towered over top of her, so she leaned back a few inches and gave him her most determined look. "So, you're saying you'll visit me at Rothgale Manor once I'm wed?"

"For what reason would a single gentleman have to visit a married woman?"

"You could bring Olivia with you when you visit. A brother chaperoning his sister would be most acceptable, his sister being one of my dearest friends."

"The fact that you're not yet Roth's wife, but are already feeling fearful over not seeing your family and friends is a clear sign that you're well aware you're about to lose your freedom. Roth rarely allowed his first three wives to leave his home, and it's doubtful he'll allow you to either. He is a tyrant, aggressive and dominating, not that you don't already know that."

"I'm aware of his nature, although I can be quite resourceful myself." She kept a stiff upper lip, although the blood still drained from her face and when she touched her cheeks, they were icy-cold. "Did you ever meet any of Roth's previous wives?"

"No, and you clearly need a drink. So do I." Winterly eased down beside her, plucked a bottle of her father's finest white wine from the basket and angled his head at her, his jaw firm, the arch of his brow high, and his long lashes rimming blue eyes which reflected the warm blue of the sky above. "Glasses," he whispered, "if you please?"

"My apologies. I'm not sure where my head is today." She rummaged through the basket and gathered two of the fluted glasses which had been wrapped in yellow and white striped cloth. She held them toward him. "I don't mean to bicker with you."

"I don't mean to either. Perhaps I've lost my head a little today too." He removed the cork with a soft *pop*, poured, then set the bottle back inside the basket. He shuffled closer then gently touched the backs of his fingers to her cheek while she still held the glasses. "Don't hide from me, Rosamonde. We've known each other a long time, far too long for you and me not to be open and honest with each other about such an important matter. Do you believe you'll be happy in your marriage with Roth?"

"I shall be happy enough, simply because I shall be able to visit my mother as often as I would like to. What more could a daughter ask for?" She truly didn't wish to get into this subject with him, but to instead enjoy the bright and sunny day. She passed him one of the glasses and sipped from her own. "Please, allow us to converse on a different subject. The cook has prepared a wonderful picnic and now that the sun is no longer hiding behind stormy clouds as it has for most of the week, we should embrace this moment."

"I would embrace it more if I was assured of your happiness." He sipped his wine, set his glass down then reached past her and plucked a yellow-and-white flower nodding its head within the grass. Waving it in front of her nose, he raised a brow. "Do you know what this flower is called?"

"Cowslip, from the primrose family."

"Correct." He plucked a purplish-blue flower from the patch next to the cowslip and handed both flowers to her. "And this one?"

"Sweet violet." She'd always adored the sweet scent of the violet flower and brought this pretty bud to her nose and breathed deep. With a smile, she murmured, "They're beautiful, so dainty and sweet smelling."

"What of that flower over there?" He gestured to several tall stalks of pink tubular flowers rising from within a patch of leaves, directly beside the trunk of the tree across from them.

"That's foxglove, but one must be careful with that flower since it can be poisonous to dogs, cats, and even humans." She arranged her skirts a little better to cover her ankles more adequately, then tucked the flowers he'd given her inside the basket, so she could press them between the pages of a book later. Keeping dried flowers was a hobby of hers.

"Yes, it is, yet look at how close the poisonous flowers of the foxglove are to us, and we are both quite at ease." He removed his greatcoat, raised one knee and loosely draped his arm over it. Another sip as he added, "The foxglove flower is deceptive. It looks attractive and is appealing, but we must learn to take all care around it. There are many things in life which can deceive the eye just as that flower does."

"I didn't realize you had such an interest in the study of plants, Winterly."

"My papa enjoyed experimenting in botany. He passed along that joy to me." He undid the lowest button on his blue silk waistcoat, where it pulled across his lap due to his raised knee, the fabric flowing over his white shirt, his gold cufflinks gleaming.

"I have an herbal garden and I enjoy pottering away in

it." She tried not to ogle his strong fingers as he played with the next button on his waistcoat.

"Your mother used to enjoy pottering away in the garden too, if I remember correctly." He indeed flicked another waistcoat button open.

"She still does. We often set a blanket out in the garden and she sits and weeds around her beloved plants. The gardener always leaves a small patch of weeds for her to remove here and there throughout the gardens, not that any of us have ever told Mother that. She thinks he has bad eyesight since he keeps missing the weeds." With the draping branches shading her, she tugged the ribbons holding her bonnet in place and set her hat beside her. The breeze whistled through, so refreshing and delightful as it lifted one of her golden locks and tickled it across her cheek. She tucked the strands back behind her ear as Olivia's giggles and the distinctive splash of a line hitting the water floated to them.

"Rosamonde." Winterly eyed her, his eyes sparkling as he gently swirled his wine in his glass. "Let's make a toast. May our friendship grow forever stronger, no matter who you're wed to."

"Yes, may it grow forever stronger." Her throat clogged up at his profound and thoughtful toast. She clinked her glass against his, then sipped slowly from the rim, the stemmed flute shaking a little in her fingers. "Mmm, this wine is delicious and glides smoothly over the tongue."

"It certainly does." He sipped his own wine, his gaze moving over her lips, his brow furrowing heavily before he snapped his gaze away.

"Is something wrong?" she asked and patted her lips to be sure she hadn't caught dirt or grit on them while fishing.

"No. Yes. No." He shook his head as if trying to clear his thoughts then gulped his wine before setting the empty glass on the grass and lying down. Resting his head on the blanket, he idly crossed his legs at the ankle and stared at the canopy overhead where the sun sprinkled through here and there. "Roth is like the foxglove flower. You'll need to take all care around him, my sweet Rosamonde."

"Roth would never endanger my life, not when he wishes for me to provide him with an heir."

"If he ever endangered your life, I'd kill him." He moved swiftly, plucking her glass from her hand then toppling her onto her back. Planting a hand over her mouth, he caught her surprised shriek with his palm.

"What are you doing?" she mumbled through his fingers. "Let me up."

"Not yet. You are bringing all my protective instincts to the fore." Half-covering her body with his, he suddenly smiled as if he'd won some kind of game between them, a secretive kind of smile lifting his lips. "Good heavens, but you have grown into a beautiful woman these past few years."

"I am a lady, sir, and you are squishing me." She plucked his fingers from her mouth. "Did you catch that mumble?"

"I did, and you're a beautiful woman with a sassy tongue and a feisty nature. I've always respected and admired that trait within you." He brushed aside tendrils of her hair sweeping across her cheeks, his touch so gentle. "Your beauty shines not only from the outside, but from deep within your heart. You have cared for your mother, been her constant companion since she lost the use of her legs, and now you intend on marrying a man who would take advantage of you. You need a husband who will appreciate your inner beauty."

"And do you know of such a man?"

"If you were permitted to enjoy a Season, you might find him without any issue at all and dare I say it, all on your own terms, without anyone else interfering in the matter." He let out a long breath, the air warm and sultry as it fanned across her cheek.

"I am out of time, Winterly." Butterflies swarmed in her belly, barely a breath whistling past her lips. He had never been so bold with her before, but oh my, as the afternoon sunshine caught on the longer ends of his chestnut brown hair and lit them a golden hue, he completely captivated her.

"Rosamonde, my sweet Rosamonde." He rubbed his cheek against her cheek, his eyes closing. "You're suddenly evoking new feelings within me which are rather unusual."

"Unusual in what way?"

"You're my best friend's little sister." He opened his eyes, his sooty lashes framing his indecently beautiful eyes.

"That doesn't explain your unusual feelings."

"Maybe my actions will." He pressed a kiss to each of her cheeks, then drew her swiftly to her feet and holding her hand, tugged her through the copse of trees. They crunched leaves and twigs beneath their feet then abruptly he pinned her against the wide trunk of a tree quite some distance from the others, his head dipping toward hers. "I need to kiss you."

"You do?"

"Yes." Without hesitation, he covered her mouth with his, and in what was certainly a defining moment, Winterly kissed her, slowly and surely.

Her heart almost catapulted from her chest and her legs certainly wobbled. She speared her fingers deep into his hair and returned his kiss with all the longing she'd always held within her heart for him. This was the man who had rescued her from a band of brigands and who had saved her and her kitten from high within the branches of a tree. As he deepened their kiss, she couldn't halt the sensuous tremor which skittered delightfully down her spine, an intriguing sensation she'd never experienced when kissing a man before. It caused a flutter to take flight low in her belly, one which pulsed through with a vivid heat that curled her toes. Nothing had ever felt so wondrously perfect, and when he slipped his tongue between her lips, even more heat flared through her, making her moan with need. Oh goodness. This was all too much, all too soon. She couldn't allow him to send her remaining good senses from her mind. She was set to wed another man, and unfortunately, not this one.

Pressing against his chest, she pushed him back. "My lord, you are not behaving as a proper gentleman should, and I'm not acting as a lady should. I do apologize if I've—"

"Don't apologize to me." He pressed one finger against her lips. "Where did you learn to kiss so beautifully?"

"I've kissed the odd man here and there, but not quite as we just kissed."

"Who exactly were these men?" He narrowed his gaze.

"Men I danced with at country balls and such. We do have gatherings out here in the wilderness, just as you have them in London, although to a much smaller degree of course."

"I'm well aware you do, but you surprised me is all." He stepped back, his brow quirking high. "So, have I now expressed to you exactly how unusual my feelings for you have suddenly become?"

"They are not feelings I can return. I am—"

The pounding of hooves drummed and the Marquess of Roth appeared atop his horse as he rode through the trees, his thinning gray hair hidden underneath his hat, his cane lying across his lap. He shot her a very narrow-eyed look as he brought his mount to a halt only a few feet away.

Winterly moved quickly in front of her and blocked her from Roth's sight.

Roth cleared his throat. "Lord Winterly, how unusual to find you here at Hillhurst Hall, and with my betrothed no less."

"I'm here for the earl and countess's house party, a yearly invitation my family receives. We are close, of course, our families that is." Winterly clasped his hands behind his back, his shoulders stiff.

From behind him, she couldn't help but touch her fingers to his clasped fingers, the slightest brush, which eased both her fear a little and his sudden stiffness. He rolled his shoulders as he eyed Roth. "I wasn't aware you were attending the party, Roth."

"Of course I am, although I'm still rather surprised at finding you here alone with my betrothed." Roth's horse snorted and reared back a step, although the marquess brought his mount quickly back under control, the reins firm in his gloved hands.

"Lady Rosamonde and I have known each other since childhood. She is a friend of mine, just as her brother is. I've now pointed out the closeness between her family and my family twice. Do I need to do so again?"

"Single gentlemen do not befriend young ladies, no matter whether their families are close or not. To do so would cause an unnecessary stir within Society and I for one am certain that the Countess of Hillhurst would never condone such a relationship between you and her daughter, a relationship whereby you feel as if you can wander about the countryside alone with her. Neither shall I condone it myself once Lady Rosamonde and I are wed." A low growl rumbled from Roth as he tried to peer around Winterly to catch her gaze. "Step forward, my lady. I wish to see you, to make certain you are well."

"My sister is very well," Avery huffed as he stepped clear of the trees and joined them, Olivia two steps behind him, Olivia's hand on her bonnet as she caught her breath.

Relief filled her and she sent her brother and Olivia a grateful smile.

"Good day, Lord Roth," Olivia said with bright eyes. "We've been expecting you."

"It doesn't appear that way to me." Roth fisted his cane.

"Oh, pfft." Olivia linked one arm with Rosamonde. "Come, my dear friend. The picnic awaits us, and we shall serve these gentlemen some delicious food."

"Yes, we shall." Rosamonde ducked her head as she allowed Olivia to walk her back through the trees toward their picnic. Good grief, what had she been thinking? Of allowing Winterly's kisses and risking Roth's ire?

Chapter 4

"It appears I was right." Avery stared into the picnic basket where he sat on the tartan blanket. "There are roast beef sandwiches in here, pickled eggs, and ham and egg pie."

"There will be dessert too. Our cook made raspberry tarts and apple pie," Rosamonde assured her brother. "Heathcoat is bringing the dessert basket from the house as we speak. He shouldn't be long."

"Wonderful." Avery winked at Rosamonde.

Winterly eased down onto the blanket, directly across from Rosamonde, while Roth secured his horse near the water's edge. The marquess knotted his reins to a low branch of a willow then strode toward them, the man sending him a very dark look as he sat next to Rosamonde.

It appeared Roth wasn't all that thrilled about having such a large party present at his proposed picnic with his betrothed. Well, too bad. And damn it, this was a frustrating time for Winterly to suddenly have such confusing feelings about a lady he'd considered Avery's little sister. She'd completely knocked him senseless with her tantalizing desirability this day.

Rosamonde set out plates of food for everyone, her blond locks rippling with soft and bright shades of gold, and when she snuck a quick look at him from under her eyelashes, he almost lost his breath. Never had he been struck silent before, but he had been now.

"This was a lovely idea of yours, Lord Roth." Rosamonde switched her gaze to Roth as she passed the marquess a plate.

"My express instructions were that you and I would enjoy a picnic." A harrumph as Roth snatched the plate from her hands. "I did not expect the rest of your house guests to accompany us."

As always the marquess was being damned rude, and Rosamonde's cheeks had flared a bright red at his crude words. Perhaps it was best if Winterly didn't look at her. Forcing himself not to say a word in response, he instead selected one of the roast beef sandwiches and allowed the hum of conversation from the others to fade into the distance, his gaze moving toward the lake.

Through the sweeping branches of the willow, crystalline blue-green waters rippled. A speckled deer emerged from the woods and trotted down to the pebbly shoreline. The animal dunked its snout into the water and drank. Out in the middle of the lake, a small island rose with a dwelling which resembled a domed Grecian temple built upon it. Avery and Rosamonde's father had commissioned the build for his countess, the temple surrounded on one side by dense trees and on the other, the shore.

In his younger years, when he'd returned from Eton with Avery for the summer holidays, he and his friend had taken a rowboat out to the island and enjoyed the peacefulness of the place. Inside under the central domed roof, artwork lined the walls, all of the pieces within painted by Lady Hillhurst who had a wonderfully artistic hand and took great pleasure in the peace and quiet of the temple in which she embraced her muse. It hadn't always been terribly quiet though, not when little Rosamonde would play with a tea set or her dolls or race about squealing with childhood exuberance.

From near the edge of the island's shoreline, a male peacock shrieked, its call echoing across the waters and its gloriously colored feathers fanning up and outward. The iridescent colors reflected blue, turquoise, and green in a vivid and artistic display that stunned the eye. The birds had been a frippery purchased by Lord Hillhurst when his wife had commented on how pretty the birds were after seeing them elsewhere. She'd adored the colors of their plumage, and her husband had promptly purchased a pair and set them upon the island for his wife's pleasure.

A female peahen plodded out from the trees surrounding the temple, pecking at the grass and plants as it foraged for food, likely nabbing an insect or a berry here and there from within the bushes. Several peachicks chased after her then scattered about the shrubbery as they too pecked. The female didn't join her male at first, not until the peacock let out an impressive musical vocalization. The male spread his train of feathers even wider and shivered them in the air as he attempted to attract his female.

His lady peahen circled closer before she finally gave her mate her back and as soon as she did, the male tucked his plumage away, swept onto her back and aligned his tail feathers overtop of his female's shorter tail.

They mated and never had he seen anything quite so simplistically beautiful.

The male had no need to attend a Season and run the gamut of the marriage mart as he himself would soon have to do once he'd seen to Olivia's future. No dilly-dallying for the peacock. The bird had no need to adhere to all of Society's rules in order to gain his heir. No, he'd have more offspring in a matter of months, more peachicks who'd eventually become fully grown and fly from the island, those birds soon seeking their own place to nest and grow their families.

As the male slid from his female's back, the crests on the top of both of the birds' heads swayed and the two of them returned to scouting the bushes for food.

The deed was all but done, which brought forth a swarm of uncomfortable thoughts surrounding the lady seated on the blanket across from him as she took a delicate bite from her sandwich. She was like a peahen, chosen by Roth to provide him solely with offspring and naught else. Roth didn't want Rosamonde for her compassionate nature, nor for her heartfelt love. He wanted her only for her ability to produce male heirs.

Rosamonde would soon be leaving a family she adored, entering into an arranged marriage, which was unfortunately quite the norm for those of the peerage where couples wed for practical, financial, or even political gain. She certainly attended to Roth dutifully during the picnic, ensuring he had plenty to eat and drink.

The marquess's manor lay only a short ride beyond the rolling hills to the north of the lake, so much closer than his own country estate which was a four-hour ride south from here. Not that he spent a great deal of time at Winterly Manor. Six months of the year he lived in London, which meant he couldn't possibly offer her what Roth currently did—daily visits with her family.

"Lord Winterly, did you wish for another sandwich?" Rosamonde eyed him expectantly, her voice a soft whisper as Roth conversed with Avery on the current bill being read in Parliament. "You're rather quiet. Is, ah, everything all right?" she continued in a soft murmur.

Olivia touched his arm as she sipped her wine. "I was going to ask the same question, brother. I've never known you to be so quiet. The temple on the island has held your attention for quite some time."

"I was reminiscing about old times." He smiled at his sister then returned his gaze to Rosamonde. "Yes, I would like another sandwich." He'd polished off his first one while watching the birds.

"What old times do you mean?" Rosamonde asked as she passed him the plate of sandwiches.

"I used to row out to the island with Avery whenever I visited. Does your mother still use her retreat for painting?" He selected one and bit into it.

"Yes, she does. Father brings her to the dock around the bend and rows out to the island with her once a week. Usually I join them, to feed the birds and such."

Two liveried footmen appeared through the trees with another basket and after Rosamonde beckoned them forward, they removed the empty basket and deposited the other. The servants milled about, stacking up used plates and serving more wine. Rosamonde set an assortment of desserts out, including viands and cheeses for those who might wish for a savory finish to their meal, of which Roth inclined his head with a silent yes when Rosamonde asked him if he wished for her to plate some of the cheeses for him.

Winterly himself accepted a slice of apple pie when Rosamonde passed him a plate since she already knew he adored apple pie. It wasn't unusual for him to crave a midnight snack, and several times while staying here, he'd snuck downstairs after everyone had gone to bed and found her in the kitchens enjoying a midnight snack as well. Apple pie. The two of them would devour slices of pie together, chatting and laughing. Now, with his dessert fork in hand, he ate a bite as he met her smiling gaze, her thoughts having clearly returned to those special moments too. The apple was deliciously sweet, the pastry light and airy, the perfect combination. "It's delicious," he told her. "As always."

"This is a beautiful spot you have here, Rosamonde." Olivia stretched out her legs, her leather-soled half boots poking out from underneath the long hem of her daffodil-yellow walking gown. His sister selected a sweet raspberry tart and nibbled delicately on it. "Perhaps we could try fishing again tomorrow since we seem to have neglected the poles."

The poles had been left on the grass, presumably where Avery and Olivia had dropped them after they'd come running to his and Rosamonde's aid.

"It might be best if we fished from one of the rowboats, rather than from the shoreline," Rosamonde declared and got a chuckle from Avery who had turned from his conversation with Roth and caught his sister's words.

"The poor fish will simply have to scatter farther from you if you do." Avery rubbed his sister's arm. "You should stick to stone-skipping."

"Of all the cheek." She tossed a slice of cheese at her brother.

Avery deftly swiped the cheese from the air and popped it into his mouth. "Or perhaps, it would be best if you gave fishing up entirely. It isn't a sport suited to you at all, dear sister."

"Catching fish in the lake is a far better sport than chasing after a helpless creature while you hunt it in the woods." Rosamonde wagged a finger at him. "I ride along on the hunts to ensure the animals get a chance to run away."

"I knew it." Avery chuckled again. "That's the first time you've admitted to the trickery though."

"Every lady needs her secrets."

"Well, as lovely as this picnic has been," Roth muttered as he stood, a huff and a puff of his chest as he nodded curtly at them all. "Do please excuse Lady Rosamonde and I. We have matters to discuss regarding our forthcoming wedding."

"Oh, we do?" Rosamonde pushed to her feet and brushed crumbs from her skirts.

"Yes, I'd like to speak to your father before this day is done."

"Of course." She sent Olivia a fretful look. "I'm sorry. Will you be able to return to the house with your brother?"

"Yes, without any issue. You go." Olivia waved her away. "We can catch up later this afternoon."

"Thank you." Rosamonde squeezed Olivia's hand and accepted Roth's arm.

The last thing Winterly wanted to do was watch Roth leading Rosamonde away, but he couldn't pull his gaze from either of them, not as Roth retrieved his horse and led his mount by the reins past them. One of the footmen followed a suitable distance behind as Roth walked along the path where the tracks of a cart cut through the grass in a direct line back toward Hillhurst Hall on the hilly rise. The two-story house held large wings off each side with stables and service quarters in behind, the home boasting over one-hundred and fifty rooms, including a lavish ballroom. It was a palatial residence, surrounded by extensive gardens. Sophisticated and stately, it had been the home to the Raven family for countless generations.

It would be where he would have to suffer watching Lord Roth and Rosamonde together during the remainder of this house party. No longer was he looking forward to even a single moment of that time.

Chapter 5

Later that evening, Rosamonde stood alone at the base of the stairs near the drawing room where her parents now entertained their guests, the chatter of voices drifting through from under the closed door. Earlier in the day when she'd returned to the hall with Lord Roth, he'd reprimanded her severely. He'd certainly been holding his tongue during their picnic because by golly, he'd been incredibly livid at finding her alone with Lord Winterly and hadn't had any issue stating so, even more so than he had at the time he'd found her.

After handing his horse to a stable hand, Roth had then marched her inside, directly into a small parlor down a side hallway where one could be assured of some peace and quiet. He'd closed the door and when she'd told him it must remain open, he'd told her quite bluntly that as an engaged couple, they could spend a few minutes alone together. It was expected, and would ensure neither of them could set their betrothal aside without causing a complete scandal for the other. He'd then demanded her earlier behavior with Winterly never be repeated again, and that should he ever find her alone with a gentleman, any gentleman, she would suffer his wrath for her disobedience.

Even now, several hours later, she could still feel the strength of his grip on her wrist and she rubbed the achy spot. Thankfully, once she'd conceded her agreement to his decree, he'd released his punishing hold on her and had allowed her to retire to her chamber for a rest.

Never had she witnessed her own father manhandling her mother in such a way, although she'd heard of husbands who could be rough with their wives. So too, once they were wed, she would be his property, which sent chills shuddering through her. He could beat her black and blue if he so desired, although she sincerely doubted he would, not when it was his wish to procure an heir from her. Perhaps she should tell her father what had transpired, but guilt ate at her. Not only would that place her father in a difficult situation, but in truth she shouldn't have been alone with Winterly in the first place, and certainly not kissing him as scandalously as she had.

It was her duty to aid her family wherever possible, which meant aligning herself in marriage with Roth. A debt remained in place, one her father couldn't repay, a fact which she shouldn't forget. The last thing she wanted was for her parents to lose any property or have to sell personal items to meet the payment of any bills.

"Lady Rosamonde!" Lord Roth strode along the upper landing overlooking the banister, his gray, flinty gaze locked on her. With a flick of his black coattails, he marched downstairs. "Wait right there. I shan't be a moment."

Even though she tried to straighten her shoulders, she couldn't help but flinch as he descended the stairs, his shoes clomping and his walking cane thumping on the polished wooden steps. As he halted in front of her, bringing with him that positively awful scent of pipe-smoke, she dipped into a curtsy and pushed a smile onto her face. "Good evening, my lord."

"You didn't join us for dinner. Why not?" Another thump of this cane, his displeasure clear to see.

"I, ah, was a little under the weather after such a long day out. I'm feeling much better now though. Thank you for inquiring about my health." She kept her smile in place, rather valiantly. When she'd missed the dinner hour due to the turmoil of the afternoon which had caused her belly to roll with unease, she'd sent her maid with a message to her parents saying that she'd be down after the dinner hour following a short rest. Thankfully, they hadn't questioned her decision to miss the meal.

Roth gripped her elbow, right over the fine blush-colored lace of her evening gown's sleeves, his gnarly fingers pinching in hard. "Come with me."

"There is no need—"

"Come." He steered her along the hallway, past the butler standing near the front door and back down another hallway within the eastern wing before urging her into the dreaded parlor where he'd been too rough with her earlier.

The parlor windows remained open, the gentle nighttime breeze swaying the burgundy drapes and golden tasseled ties securing the thick folds of fabric back. This time he left the door open, then stepped away from her and rested a hand on the mantel over the fireplace stacked with wood ready to be lit should the fire be needed. A lone candle flickered from atop a side table, while a basket of her mother's embroidery threads were tucked away next to the burgundy padded corner armchair. She gestured to the drinks' cabinet. "Would you care for a brandy?"

"No." A snappy return. "Has your father made you aware of the conversation he and I had earlier this afternoon while you were resting in your chamber?"

"He didn't." The dreaded chills returned.

"Then I shall inform you. The funds set aside for your dowry—twenty thousand pounds to be exact—will be paid to me as due, although I've kindly offered to reduce your father's debt by the same figure." A glint lit his eyes, an unsavory glint. "Call it my wedding gift to you."

"I see." She clasped her hands behind her back and tried heartedly hard to reinsert her usual calm control. Allowing him to believe she had no backbone wasn't acceptable. "My lord, your generosity knows no bounds. I graciously thank you."

"His debt to me is rather substantial, twenty thousand pounds being a miniscule amount compared to the full sum of the loan. A hundred and fifty thousand pounds, in case you weren't aware."

"Oh my." She clasped a hand to her mouth, having had no idea the loan had been that high. Such an exorbitant amount. Father would have to sell unentailed property to meet such a huge debt. He'd already told her he had several investments on the go, but none he'd be able to cash in. The profits from those investments wouldn't be available for five years, which meant she was stuck in her current predicament with no other way out.

"With your father's debt being rather substantial, so now is your debt to me, a debt which must also be repaid." His gaze swept lasciviously down her neck to the low cut neckline of her gown, his appraisal of her breasts clear to see as he smirked.

She shuddered with revolt. Desperately she wished to cover herself up, but instead she maintained her position with her hands clasped behind her back.

Booted footsteps echoed down the hallway and she closed her eyes and prayed that it would be Avery, then she just as swiftly prayed it wouldn't be. Her brother had always been one of her staunchest protectors and ever since Father had announced her betrothal in his study, her brother had been pushing her at every opportunity for an explanation as to why she'd so swiftly agreed to the match. Of course, he understood she'd done so in order for the alliance which would benefit their family, but he knew deep down there was more to it. What he wasn't aware of was the loan, or that Roth had been set to wed their mother all those years ago. If Father wished to speak of either issue to Avery then he would. It was most certainly not her place to share the details, otherwise she might very well be causing more problems than she ever would in solving them. Meanwhile, the marquess was right. She now owed him a great debt, one representing the sum of twenty thousand pounds, a debt that could only be repaid by birthing him a son.

"Look at me, Lady Rosamonde." A command from Roth as he stepped closer, the smoky scent surrounding him clogging her throat. With one knobby finger under her chin, his nail scraping her skin, he leaned in. "You will provide me with—"

"Do pardon me. I hope I'm not interrupting anything important." Winterly stood in the doorway, his nostrils flaring as he glared at Roth. In his fisted hand he gripped a sealed letter and he extended it toward Roth. "A message from Rothgale Manor. I was walking through the front foyer when your coachman arrived with it. Your servant awaits outside for your answer."

Roth continued to stare at her, then snorted as he shot Winterly a glare. Slowly, Roth eased back a step, his fingernail scraping her skin before he lowered his hand and turned toward Winterly and accepted the letter. Roth slid his thumb under the seal and broke it, removed his eyeglasses from his jacket pocket and unfolded the paper. Wandering closer to the light of the candle, he read the missive with deep furrows lining his weathered brow.

More footsteps and Avery stepped into the parlor, his gaze moving from Winterly to Roth, then to her then Winterly again. Her brother didn't utter a word as he moved directly to her side, as if he were aware she required his strength at this moment.

Winterly moved swiftly to her other side and she struggled to breathe under the joint force of their commanding presence. Still, she needed them both in this moment and no matter she hadn't been able to convey that to either of them with words, they'd still somehow sensed her need and understood all the same.

Clearing her throat, she arched a brow at Roth. "Is everything well at Rothgale, my lord?"

"As well as can be." He folded the letter, slid it into his

pocket and tucked his eyeglasses away. A stare down his nose at her. "Unfortunately, one of my stable lads was found half an hour ago trampled to death by a horse."

"Oh, good grief." Shocked, she fluttered a hand over her mouth. "I'm so sorry."

He shrugged. "The lad was deaf and mute, which is likely the cause of the issue. Still, I need to return home and see to matters. I'll return tomorrow for the hunt."

"Take as long as you need." Her heart heaved for the lad's family.

A dip of his head, his gaze still on hers as he stepped up to her. "Remember my words, my lady." Which sounded entirely like a threat as he snapped a fierce look at Winterly then her brother before marching out the door.

Once the echo of his footsteps trailed away, Avery swung around and eyed her. "Remember what words? Speak of them now."

"I can handle Roth." Raising a hand to hold her brother from his coming spiel, she added, "You know how strong and resilient I can be."

"You are my sister, my only sister. I will protect you, with my own life if need be." He searched her gaze. "Tell me what the hell Roth is holding over you, what he's holding over Father."

"I'm not permitted to speak on the issue." The truth, which wouldn't placate her brother one little bit, so she reached up on her toes and kissed his cheek. "I love you, Avery, although I'm a lady who doesn't need to hold affection or even have tender feelings for my forthcoming husband."

"Yes, you do."

"No, I don't. Such emotions aren't expected when marriages take place within our Society. We are simply fortunate that our parents love each other dearly, that we've seen how wonderful such a union can be. I'm well aware I won't have that, a fact I have accepted. You need to accept it too."

"You still need more than what Roth can ever offer—"

"I would even go so far as to say any hint of emotion within a marriage could be considered very unfashionable amongst the *ton*," she muttered as she interrupted her brother. "Lord Roth holds no great sentiment for me, but that shall simply ensure an uncomplicated marriage. His only requirement is that I provide him with an heir, while my only requirement is for a husband who resides close to Hillhurst Hall, and a husband who will allow me to visit my family's home so that I might remain as Mother's companion for as long as I possibly can. I can't leave Mother, not when she needs me."

"Lord Roth mightn't need to engage his heart with his next marchioness, but you will slowly wither and die away should you not be permitted to engage yours. You would be better off choosing say—" Her brother raised his hands in supplication then pointed at Winterly. "Winterly would be a far better match for you than anyone I know. Winterly Manor is only a four-hour ride from here."

"Avery." Frustration thrummed through her. "Winterly isn't looking for a wife."

"Not many men are until it becomes a necessity."

She growled under her breath then shook her head at Winterly. "Please, ignore my brother. He is half out of his mind."

"I'm not out of my mind at all." Excitement suddenly ringed Avery's tone as he clasped Winterly's shoulder. "Gads, why didn't I think of it sooner? You need to wed eventually, so why not right now? Beat Roth to the mark, so to say."

"Oh goodness, are you trying to force your friend into offering for my hand?" Shocked, she swatted Avery on the arm. "You are even more out of your mind than I thought."

"If not Winterly, then cast your net wider." Avery gripped her shoulder, just as he still clasped Winterly's.

"That's impossible. If I broke my betrothal to Roth, my actions would cause a scandal, which would impact our entire family. Mother doesn't need that kind of worry when her focus must remain on her recovery. Her toes now tingle, an improvement in sensation since she began using the water therapy the doctor advised." Father had commissioned the building of a small indoor bathing pool at the rear of the house where glass windows on one side allowed Mother to view the gardens as she rested in the warm water while her maid moved Mother's legs in a gentle kicking motion. Indeed, those sessions in the pool had stimulated her senses. "Are you aware of that?"

"Excuse me while I cut into your argument." Winterly stepped in between her and Avery, then with a firm nudge toward the door, he steered Avery in that direction. "Give me a moment alone with your sister, if you will."

"Good man. That's a superb answer to this atrocious dilemma. Spend some time with my sister and see if you can bring her around to my idea." Avery's eyes shone bright, his smile wide as he clapped Winterly on the back. "I'll be down the hallway. If you intend on proposing, then take your time. I'll ensure no one interrupts you."

"Avery don't you dare leave us alone." She hurried after him, but her brother stepped through the door and closed it firmly behind him. With a huff, she spun around and turned on Winterly. "I don't need your pity."

Winterly actually had the audacity to smile as he lowered himself onto one knee before her. "Rosamonde—"

"No. My answer is no. Please, you must stand and—well, I'm not accepting any possible offer of marriage from you, no matter that you kissed me down by the lake and curled my toes when you did."

"Your kisses curled my toes too, my seductive Rosamonde." Still on one knee, he caught her hand and held it captive in his, his gaze mesmerizing as he looked at her. "Avery is right. I do eventually need to wed, so why not now?"

"I said up."

"My dear lady, I have had the pleasure of knowing you since you were but a child in short skirts. You've always been a sweet young lass, a bit too mischievous during your youth, but you've got a delightfully pleasant countenance, are sensible and intelligent and can speak three languages fluently."

"Four languages." She tugged her hand back and crossed her arms. "You must cease this charade immediately."

"I apologize, four languages fluently." He rose from one knee back to his full height. "You are also adept at entertaining and socializing among polite society, can play the pianoforte and sing as beautifully as a sparrow from a tree top. You would make a wonderful female companion, a wife to comfort me when I have need of your gentle touch, and"—he lowered his tone as he dipped his head to her ear—"a passionate nature which I intend on encouraging at every possible opportunity."

"Now you've gone too far." Scorching heat flared across her cheeks, his words beyond scandalous and panting a little, she pressed the backs of her hands to her heated cheeks.

"No, I've not yet gone far enough." He grinned, rather rakishly. "I wasn't aware until my arrival here at Hillhurst Hall of exactly how much I desired you."

"It's not desire you feel but pity."

"Which brings me to the question I must ask you," he uttered, as if she hadn't just interrupted him. "Lady Rosamonde Raven, I wish for you to be my countess. Will you do me the great honor of accepting my proposal and marrying me?"

"No. The answer is still a resounding no." Hopefully now he'd put this teasing interlude behind them. She tapped one foot, crossed her arms. "My lord, your house party etiquette is atrocious. You do not propose willy-nilly to a lady simply because you don't approve of the man she will soon wed, or because her brother doesn't approve of the man, but approves of you instead."

"You can't marry Roth." He crossed his own arms, matching her stance exactly. "I also insist you cease calling me 'my lord'. When we're alone, you must call me by first name."

"I don't know your first name, and Lord Roth asked that I no longer repeat my earlier behavior of today, that I be found alone with a gentleman, particularly you, otherwise I will suffer his wrath for any disobedience. I must ask you to honor his decree and no longer speak to me again in private."

"It's Richard, my first name."

"I'm quite serious. My lord, it has been a pleasure to spend time with you today, but alas, it can be no more. I must join my family and yours in the drawing room. I wish you a good evening for what remains of the night." She grasped her skirts and lowered into a graceful curtsy, the loose curls her maid had piled atop her head brushing forward across her cheeks.

She swept to the door and—

He beat her there, his palm pressed against the dark wood over the top of her head.

Taking an unsteady breath, she turned around and met his striking blue gaze.

The gaze of a man who wouldn't be deterred.

The gaze of a man she'd always admired.

The gaze of her childhood hero.

Chapter 6

"We haven't finished our conversation yet." There wasn't a chance Winterly would allow Rosamonde to leave, not when she believed his proposal had been spoken out of pity. Pity had never existed between them and he doubted it ever would. No, there was far more at stake here for both of them. Of course, he truly did desire her, that emotion having roared to life this day, of which it would no longer abate.

Pressing both palms on the closed door either side of her head, he leaned in until the lapels of his evening jacket brushed the fine blush-colored lace overlaying the silk of her gown's neckline. Perhaps a little intimidation was in order, so she understood exactly where the two of them now stood.

Clearing his throat, he looked deep into her eyes. "Rosamonde, I have known you for years, just as you've known me. I'm always in full command of my actions and emotions, but with you today, any command I've had over myself has been swept away by the intensity of my need for you. You are a woman proper, and I proposed because I'm also fully capable of making my own decisions. I want to take you as my wife."

Breath stuttering, she tipped her chin up as she searched his gaze. With the long, slim line of her neck fully revealed, her rosy lips parting as if she were fully prepared to counter his words, he waited as she opened her mouth, closed it, then opened it again. More stuttered breathing, her gaze on his lips, which caused fierce desire to shoot straight to his nether regions. His cock pressed painfully hard against the opening flap of his black breeches and he groaned at the swift intensity of passion she once more roused within him.

Damn it all, but he wanted to kiss her again, to taste her sweet lips. By the lake, her eager kisses had nearly undone him, her sweet raspberry and vanilla scent clinging to her, just as it clung to her now. That sweet scent filled his senses and taunted him, as it would surely continue to taunt him every day that was to come.

With her breasts rising and falling rapidly, she licked her lips, which drew his gaze directly to her mouth. He leaned in closer still, his desire roaring forth. Never had he experienced such a defining moment as this in his life. If he allowed her to walk away from him now, he might never get her back. A certain truth. He had to ensure she embraced this moment just as he currently did.

He took one of her hands in his and pressed her palm flat against his pounding heartbeat, directly over the dark silk of his waistcoat inlaid with gold thread. He waited for her to say something, do something, and when she curled her fingers inward and held on to him even more tightly, he touched his nose to her nose.

Dark and dangerous sensations swirled through him.

Those emotions weren't only of passion, but of far more complicated feelings. The thought of her marrying Roth and starting a family with the man had caused an ache to grip his heart in a fierce hold. He truly wanted her as his wife, and since this might be his last chance to convince her that they needed to be together, he had to take the bull by the horns.

Yes, he intended to get a little underhanded in his coming actions, but he had everything to lose if he didn't act fast. Moving swiftly, he caught her other hand and wound it around his neck, then he licked her lower lip and whispered, "You are so beautiful. I want to ravish you."

"You are making me lose my mind, for the second time today." She speared her fingers deep into his hair.

"You've already made me lose mine." He covered her mouth with his, wanting only to share his breath with her and have hers fill his lungs in return and she granted his wish, her breath mingling seductively with his as it whispered across his tongue.

He kissed her, their tongues dancing together, their mouths moving in a heated duel as desire roared through his blood and hardened his cock even further. He shifted and pressed his hips against her hips, every curve of her soft body now molded to his. When she gasped and moaned, he greedily demanded more. Gently cupping the weight of one of her breasts in his hand, he flicked his thumb across her nipple poking through the thin blush-colored cloth of her bodice. Caressing and stroking her lush flesh, he deepened their kiss and muttered, "You feel so good in my arms, Rosamonde."

"We shouldn't be doing this." She moaned in return and once more opened her mouth fully under his.

He welcomed the dark intimacy their position now afforded them. Slowly sweeping his lips downward, he trailed kisses down the graceful line of her neck and along the upper swells of her breasts.

"Oh, Richard." She slid one hand inside his waistcoat and spread her fingers across the thin white linen of his ruffled shirt. "I've never felt this kind of passion in my life. Is it always like this between a man and a woman?"

"No, and it's a passion neither of us will be able to sate with mere kisses tonight. I need to touch more of you." He tipped her chin up and captured her mouth with brutal deliberateness. Over and over, he kissed her as if it might be his last chance to do so. A reality at the moment, if he couldn't convince her to accept his offer of marriage.

"Touch me again, as you touched me before," she breathed as she broke their kiss and pressed his hand more firmly over her silk-covered breast. "Right here."

With his mouth covering hers, he kissed her deeply as he pinched and plucked at her nipple. The feel and taste of her drugged his senses, his need for her an unstoppable beat in his blood. He craved her, quite simply and forcibly, the intensity of his need unable to be extinguished. He dragged his hand down her side, clutched her skirts and lifted them. With the fabric bunched over his hand, he stroked the bare skin of her outer thigh, right above her garter. He should be making allowances for her youth and inexperience, but her soft moans urged him on.

He stroked the silky softness of her flesh then moved with boldness toward her mound and cupped her intimately. She whimpered, trembling in his arms and a need unlike anything he'd ever known before surged through him. He teased her entrance with a sensual slide of his fingers, and she grasped his shoulders and clung to him.

"Don't stop," she demanded.

"I won't." Pushing one finger deep between her folds and into the exquisite tightness of her channel, he captured her mouth again and kissed her until they both panted for air. "My sweet seductress, you're so wet and tight and perfect. Once we are wed, I intend on burying my cock within you, as deeply as I can."

"I need more." She dug her nails deeper into his shoulders. "Goodness, give me more."

"I will." He intended to deliver all that she needed. He added a second finger and swirled deep inside her with a loving caress, and she widened her legs farther and when he rested his thumb on her nub and stroked that tiny bud which would bring her pleasure, she jerked her hips, her eyelids fluttering closed and her lips parting.

He caught her cry with his mouth and kissed her as tremors shuddered through her and only once they had subsided did he move his hand from her heat and allow her skirts to fall back in a soft ripple of silk to the floor. As she opened her eyes, he smiled at her. "You're so beautiful, astoundingly beautiful. I want to make you come again and again at my hand."

"I've touched myself there before as I've bathed, but never have I experienced such overwhelming sensations as I did just now with your fingers inside me." She searched his gaze. "What about you? How does a man come?"

"Since I'm in a rather randy state at present and I'm fairly certain I won't be able to walk out of here without doing something about that state first, then you're about to see." He flicked a handkerchief from his top jacket pocket, unbuttoned the flap of his breeches and covered his shaft with the cloth. Arching a brow, he smiled at her. "Do you wish to watch me come?"

"Yes. Yes, please, yes." She leaned back against the door, her chest rising and falling fast once more, her hungry gaze on his shaft. "What's your appendage called?"

"A penis or a cock." He hadn't yet allowed her a good look at his manhood, but now he removed the cloth and as her eyes widened on the sight of his rigid staff saluting her high, he couldn't help but grin. "I would like it immensely if you aided me in coming."

"How?" With one shaky hand, she hovered her fingers over the head, which was turning a vivid shade of purple under the pressure contained within it.

"Wrap your fingers right around me, like so." He caught her hand and curled her fingers around the width of him.

"Oh my, your penis is rather hard and firm, yet also smooth too. How unexpected." A mischievous twinkle lit her eyes as she slowly glided her hand up to the head then back down to the base. "Like the finest velvet, you feel so silky."

"You're doing a wonderful job of aiding me." With the cloth over the top, he covered her hand and moved her fingers in a deeper stroke and as she released a soft moan, he couldn't help but release one too.

"I like touching you." She pressed her lips to his lips, her kiss sweetly delicious, her hand moving faster with perfectly timed firmness.

Heat flared at the base of his spine and sizzled around to the front and without any further aid, he throbbed, his seed pulsing from him. It splashed the cloth, hot and wet and thick and as she gentled her touch, he slowly came back down from the heights of ecstasy she'd taken him to.

Carefully, slowly, he removed the cloth, tucked it away in his pocket and secured the front flap of his breeches.

She leaned back against the door, her eyes crinkling at the corners as she smiled. "Well, I believe we're now in a quandary, Richard."

"There shall be no quandary at all, not when I intend on speaking to your father, of asking him for your hand in marriage."

"My father is the one who wishes for me to wed Roth." She gulped, her throat working. "I haven't been able to speak to Avery about this, but I trust you. There is a large loan, one my father can't repay to Roth, not for a number of years."

"How large?"

"A hundred and fifty thousand pounds."

"That's a hefty sum." His breath whistled out from between his lips.

"Yes, which is why I must marry Roth, even after this lovely interlude of ours."

"Rosamonde—"

"No. What we just had was a few stolen moments in time. I can't disappoint my father. He's relying on me to wed Roth and ensure he doesn't lose any of his unentailed holdings." Tears pooled in her eyes and two escaped and streaked down her cheeks. "You mustn't make this any harder for me than it already is."

"I am not a man who will easily step aside, whether there is a hundred and fifty thousand pounds involved or two hundred thousand. I give you my word that I will do my damnedest to aid you and your family in finding a solution so that you and I may be together." He wiped her tears away then with a curt nod, stepped back so he didn't attempt to take her all over again.

"Please, this thing between us can never be anything more than what it has already been."

"No, only mere moments ago you came alive at my hand and you will continue to burn for me, just as I will burn for you. There can be no retreat from what now simmers between us." Certainly not for him. He would dream of her day and night until he could have her again.

She stared at him, rather helplessly, her hands rising, her palms pressed against his chest. "I've been reckless, wild and improper, but that doesn't mean—"

"It means everything to me." He lowered to one knee once more. "Lady Rosamonde, I would ask you this question a hundred and fifty thousand times, but I pray I need only ask it once more. Will you do me the great honor of accepting my proposal and marrying me? And be warned, should you say no, then I'll simply toss you over my shoulder and cart you away to Gretna Green. I won't accept any other answer, other than yes."

Chapter 7

"You are being unreasonable." Rosamonde couldn't fathom why Winterly would wish to marry her. Yes, she had adored his touch, as he had adored hers, but that didn't mean a marriage was possible between them.

"You don't want passion in your future marriage? Love? The possibility of adventure around every corner?" he asked her. "I can offer you all of that and so much more."

"Richard, you cannot speak of holding love for me when before today you hadn't even considered offering for my hand. We have both acted in a crazed manner, earlier today and of course just now."

He narrowed his gaze as he scrutinized her, which became an unbearably long scrutinization as long and precious seconds ticked away. Finally, he rose from one bent knee and cradled her face in his hands. "You are right in that before today I hadn't considered a future between the two of us, but the crazed manner in which we have both acted is certainly strong proof that intense emotions exist between us. I cannot simply walk away, not now, not after touching you the way I have. What must I say to convince you that we should be together?"

"If you truly feel any love for me at all, you wouldn't ask me to leave my home, to live so far away from my loved ones. You don't even reside at Winterly Manor for more than a few months of the year."

"I spend six months in the country and six months in London, that is true, but perhaps it's time for me to change that. I need only remain in town while parliament is in session. The remainder of the year we could both reside either at my country estate, or here. I have no issue spending time under your father's roof. Perhaps your parents could even stay with us at Winterly Manor when they desire a change of scenery."

"I could never expect you to be forced into giving up so much in order to accommodate my needs."

"That's what marriage is all about, or at least that's what my papa taught me before his passing. Like you, I come from a home where my parents loved each other dearly, where they both gave equally of themselves so that they could always remain together."

"Yet if I ever truly showed you the same love that you're offering me, then I would step away right now and give you your freedom. I would never allow you to suffer the scandal which will surely rear its ugly head should I break my betrothal with Roth." She moved away and rested her hands on the windowsill. Outside, stars twinkled in the night sky, the moon hidden behind thin clouds which floated past, but which still allowed the gentle golden glow of the moon to shine through here and there. Such an uplifting sight, yet she'd never felt less uplifted in her life. The door closed quietly with a snick and when she turned, he was gone.

He wouldn't have given up though. Winterly wasn't a man to set aside a challenge tossed at him, and she'd certainly laid down a challenge this very night.

She would need to bolster her strength against him tomorrow, otherwise she'd never be able to move forward with her life and accept it wasn't headed toward the man who had saved her as a child and it appeared, now wished to save her again. Her destiny had been set, and it didn't lead to Richard Trentbury, the Earl of Winterly. It led to the Marquess of Roth.

**

It had been a long night when Rosamonde awoke the next morning. Quite late since she'd tossed and turned for several hours before finally falling asleep, her thoughts consumed by an enticing man who had always been her hero, a man who'd brought her great passion last night with his gentle and loving touch.

With her nightgown wrapped around her legs and her hair a tangled mess across her pillow, she heaved a sigh at the heavy weight pressing down on her heart. Above her head, the yellow canopy of her bedcurtains swayed. If only her father had never borrowed funds from Roth, that a debt never existed between them, although such thoughts were nonsensical and she needed to accept the truth of her current situation. She was set to wed Lord Roth and expected to do her duty by him. In truth, she'd longed for children this past year or two, to start a family of her own.

That desire had stirred within her the day when she'd peered down through the branches of a tree at the end of her driveway and spied Winterly at the base with his hands on his hips, his gaze narrowed on her. Avery had been standing beside him, but it was only Winterly who'd taken her attention. Unfortunately she'd been hanging perilously halfway up a tree while trying to rescue her wee kitten. She'd borrowed her brother's breeches, which had been the only adequate attire she'd been able to find so she might scramble up the tree and fetch Marmalade down without alerting the entire household to her pet's misadventure. Father had already issued a final warning that if she couldn't get the kitten to behave, then it would have to go. Winterly had asked her what on earth she was doing, and when she'd pointed to the kitten on the uppermost branch of the tree, he'd heaved himself up until he'd reached her. Once he'd rescued the kitten, she'd beamed as all had finally felt right in her world. He unfortunately had scolded her for the risk she'd taken with her life, which had made her get stroppy and state her mind rather clearly in return.

That day now seemed like a lifetime ago.

A lifetime in which her world had turned upside down.

A world she must still exist within, wed to a man who'd never treated her with an ounce of kindness. Roth never would either. He was condescending, abrupt, and arrogant. There also wasn't a chance she could ever change him, not when he was too set in his ways.

Pushing her yellow and cream bedcovers back, she swung her legs over the side of her bed and rose. She plodded across the polished floorboards to her window and swept her cream and yellow floral drapes back. She touched a finger to the windowpane where sunlight streamed across it, the warmth of the new day slowly penetrating through to her. At least the weather would be fine today for the hunt, and hopefully it would remain fine for the entire week ahead.

Outside, Lady Winterly and Olivia strolled about the manicured gardens, both of them taking a turn along the meandering pathway which led to the fishpond beyond the trees where she'd played often as a child. Mother's roses bloomed everywhere, a bright splash of pretty pinks, yellows, and creams as the buds burst forth. With her parasol shading her head, Olivia waved to someone up ahead then hurried forward in her plum colored riding habit and beamed as she caught up to a man who stepped around a tall landscaped hedge with her cat in his hands. Not any man either. Winterly.

Her childhood hero removed his hat and engulfed his sister in his arms, as if they hadn't just seen each other the day before. He petted Marmalade before setting her cat gently on the grass, then lifted his head and tipped his gaze toward her window on the upper floor.

No.

She ducked to the side and plastered her back against the wall.

Heat flushed her cheeks as she took herself to task.

Standing at her window in her nightgown staring at a gentleman was beyond scandalous. She needed to cease such atrocious behavior. If he'd seen her, she'd have a lot to answer for.

A quick ring of the bell, and she summoned her maid, Mary, whom she shared with Mother.

Mary knocked and entered, an apron tied about her waist and a frilly white cap atop her head. The lass set to work readying her bath, which was filled with steaming pails of hot water by two lads who soon arrived. After the boys had left, Mary closed the door and added a swirl of her favorite raspberry and vanilla scented oil to the bathwater.

She disrobed and stepped into the tub, swiftly washed her hair, soaped her body, then not wanting to dawdle, rose to her feet and got swamped in the drying cloth her maid held out. Mary gestured for her to sit in the patch of sunshine while she dried her locks. Wrapped in her dressing gown, she seated herself, and Mary brushed her hair until the golden strands fluttered softly into a glittering fall down her back. Her maid carefully arranged her hair into an elegantly braided headband that swept around her crown with curls bobbing free from a top knot. She created a soft center part at her forehead, then added the finishing touches with intricate curls brushing her cheeks.

Her maid aided her in dressing and once clothed in her new sky-blue riding habit made by her modiste for this very hunt, she stepped in front of her tall-standing cheval mirror and turned from side to side to admire the long, clean lines of her habit. The fitted jacket followed her curves, tucking in nicely at her waist and flaring over her hips, while the hem of her skirts brushed the floorboards with a short train at the back. With her wide-brimmed hat in her hand, she twirled in a full circle, her mood lightening and the heavy weight of the night before finally lifting from her heart. She'd always adored galloping across the fields, the wind rushing by and the crisp country air invigorating her. She also enjoyed making more noise than necessary so as to warn the animals being hunted that they'd soon be found if they didn't scatter or hide.

After pinning her matching sky-blue hat in place, she took a morning tray at her side table. After enjoying a hot bread roll smothered in jam, along with a cup of tea, she laced her half boots, pulled on her riding gloves and left her chamber. She trod downstairs and at the base of the stairwell, rounded the corner as their butler strode toward her with a silver platter and a folded note upon it.

A dip of his head as he extended the platter. "For you, Lady Rosamonde, from Lord Roth. A messenger arrived from Rothgale Manor only a few minutes ago."

"Oh, thank you." She tucked her riding crop under one arm before accepting the missive. "How are his lordship and her ladyship this morning?"

"The earl is showing the Worthington and the Bellview families about the stables, so they might choose which horses they wish to ride for the hunt. They arrived an hour ago and shall be staying for the duration of the day. The countess can be found on the garden bench underneath the arbor where she has a good view of her guests and the planned activities. Lady Winterly has chosen to sit out the hunt and is keeping the countess company."

"Is the countess warm enough?" She always fretted when her mother chose to sit outside, particularly when she never noticed if her legs had become too chilled. "Someone must keep a close eye on her."

"Lady Winterly has the countess swaddled in blankets, and a footman remains close by."

"Wonderful. All sounds in order." Her mother adored

having Flora's family here, this house party and this week of activities always enthusing her very soul. "Please, ensure you serve the countess and Lady Winterly tea, immediately."

"I shall do so now." A nod of Simmonds' head and their ever-efficient butler disappeared toward the kitchens.

"There you are, my dear sister." Smiling, Avery strode toward her in blue breeches and a matching riding jacket, his white cravat knotted at his neck. He brushed a kiss across her cheek. "Winterly asked if you'd be joining us for the hunt, of which I informed him that of course you would. Roth also hasn't yet arrived, although one of his servants just delivered a note." He tipped his head toward the note in her hand. "Is that it?"

"Yes, and I wish to speak to you about Winterly." She needed to set her brother straight on her decision to turn Winterly's proposal down, as well as to explain why. Since Winterly now knew of the loan, she didn't doubt her brother would soon become aware of it too. They were the best of friends and had never withheld any secrets from each other. "Might I have a word with you in private?"

"Of course. Does the library suit?" He motioned with one hand toward the open library door only a few steps away.

"It certainly does." She led the way, dropped her crop and the missive on the side table, then crossed to the square-cut window framed with deep blue curtains. She leaned one hand on the windowsill as a pretty bird trilled from the branch of the sycamore only a few feet away. Bright sunshine and clear blue skies prevailed. Facing her brother, she clasped her hands in front of her, fully prepared to state her mind. "Avery, I need you to know that I do appreciate your concern regarding my forthcoming marriage to Roth, and even though my marriage to him is an arranged one, there are still many aspects to it which suit me. There is also the fact that I must abide by Father's request, as any diligent daughter should do. That being the case, I turned down Winterly's proposal last night."

"Winterly told me you did. He also made me aware of the loan, of which I confronted Father about. We spoke in his study earlier this morning." He rested one shoulder against a shelf of leather-bound books, his brow furrowing deeply. "Should you not wed Roth, Father will need to settle the loan immediately since Roth has made it quite clear that would happen. Unfortunately, Father isn't able to come up with the funds needed, not for five years when he can use the profit from his ventures to settle the hundred and fifty thousand pound debt. There is also the matter of your dowry, which reduced the debt by twenty thousand pounds."

"Yes. Roth has kindly offered to reduce Father's debt by the amount of my dowry." She straightened her shoulders. "Roth has called that concession his wedding gift to me."

"I had no idea that all of this was why you were so adamant in your decision to marry the man. I'm rather grateful that Winterly managed to bring all of this to my attention, and that Father has now spoken of the situation to me. I've also told Father he must inform Mother as well. We can't hide that kind of information from her."

"Is Father mad at me for speaking of all of this?"

"Of course not. In fact, I'd even say he's relieved that

he no longer has to bear the burden of this secret on his own."

"I must also consider Mother's needs though."

"Should you wed a man like Winterly who resides in London for several months of the year, living farther away than either you or Mother wished for, then that might perhaps be a good thing." Her brother stepped forward and rested his hands on her shoulders, his gaze intent. "It would certainly encourage Mother to travel, to accept that her injury can't keep her housebound forever. For goodness' sake, six years have passed, and she hasn't even been beyond the nearby village in all that time. Mother used to adore London and all the activities of the Season."

"True." She had to concede that point, that they had been making it far too easy for Mother to remain within the boundary of their property. Guilt swamped her and dipping her gaze to her feet, she scuffed one booted toe back and forth. "I still have to marry Roth though. The loan remains glaringly in place."

"It does, but after Father and I spoke, we asked Winterly to join our meeting."

"What did the three of you speak about?" If Winterly had admitted to touching her intimately, doing so would cause more problems than it ever would in resolving any. She held her breath as she waited for her brother to answer.

"Winterly insisted that we need to find a hundred and fifty thousand pounds, immediately, otherwise he'll cart you off to Gretna Green and to hell with Roth." Fire sparked in her brother's eyes. "I've never seen Winterly so beset with such intense emotions before, which means he and I have agreed to ride to London to source the funds needed to repay the loan. We shall do whatever is needed to procure the amount required so Father can repay Roth. Winterly has a few ideas, and we'll come up with a sound plan and answer to our problems as we travel. Father certainly insisted that no dash to Gretna Green would be needed or desired. He said that once he has the funds in hand and has passed them along to Roth, that he will break the betrothal, and once any resulting scandal has quietened down, then with his blessing you may accept Winterly's proposal."

"Father has truly conceded to this idea?"

"He has."

She fluttered a hand over her mouth, butterflies abounding in her belly. "What if you and Winterly can't source the funds? Roth has already set the wedding date for the end of the month. I have three weeks left in which he must be repaid and my betrothal subsequently broken."

"Winterly and I are both determined to return within that time. Two weeks should be all we need, not three."

"That is true." Winterly stood in the open doorway then closed the door behind him, a faint blue-black shadow of stubble darkening his usually cleanshaven jaw, her precious cat cradled in his arms once more.

"Are you well?" she asked, searching his gaze.

"I didn't sleep last night since this issue consumed all my thoughts."

"I'm sorry."

"Don't let my lack of sleep worry you." He lowered Marmalade onto the corner wingchair before stalking toward her. He halted only a step away, his fists clenching at his sides as if he grappled to withhold himself from touching her. He sent her brother a sharp look at which Avery nodded and strode to the door.

"Avery, wait." She rushed across and grabbed ahold of her brother's arm. "You can't leave us alone. Winterly loses all rational thought when you do, and so do I."

"I'll be directly outside the door, and I'll leave Marmalade here to chaperone you. You two have five minutes in which to come to an agreement." Her brother left and closed the door with a quiet snick behind him.

Winterly pulled the drapes across the window, the library darkening from one second to the next.

"Stay right where you are." She swayed back and bumped into the ladder used to reach the upper rows of books, except her earl didn't abide by her request at all. He was there in front of her, catching her around her waist and holding her steady.

"Say yes," he whispered.

"What if you can't procure the funds and return before the end of the month? It is a distinct possibility, no matter what you say."

"You must trust that I will, and please, you must also say yes."

"Exactly what is your question?"

"I must take every precaution possible with you before leaving for London. Avery and I shall be leaving tomorrow morning rather than today. That's because I need you to agree to my coming request."

"Which is?"

"Tonight, once all is quiet in the house, sneak away with me to Gretna Green. It is naught but a three-hour ride north from here. We can make the journey and return before dawn. Marry me in secret, without telling another soul. No one is to know what we've done, not even Avery."

"Father has already told Avery that no dash to Gretna Green would be needed or desired. He said that once the loan was repaid and my betrothal then broken, once any resulting scandal has quietened, then with his blessing I may accept your proposal."

"I was at the meeting and I am aware of what your father said, but Roth is known to be aggressive, whether that be in his business or personal dealings, and I shall be gone for twelve to fourteen days. I can't leave without knowing I've given you all the protection I can, which I can only do by making you my wife. I can't lose you, Rosamonde. I won't lose you. I'll never allow that to happen."

"I understand your worry but—"

"No buts." He pressed a finger to her lips as her cat curled between their legs. "We need never speak of the vows we take in secret. They shall only be made as a precaution and I shall lock the paperwork away."

"Do you wish to consummate these coming vows?"

"I don't want to risk getting you with child, not when it could be months yet until we have an actual wedding day. Certainly, the last thing I want for either of us is to be buried in scandal or shunned from Society. Once your engagement to Roth is broken, I want to see you enjoy a Season in London, to have your mother and father in town with you. I need to be able to court you properly, as a man does when he is smitten with his lady." He dipped his head closer, brushed his nose against her cheek and whispered in her ear, "Even though these are extenuating circumstances we currently find ourselves in, you deserve all I can offer you."

"Richard, you've offered me more than I could already even hope for." She didn't care about having a Season, only in having her family around her. "Yes, my answer is yes. I will marry you."

"In secret?"

"Absolutely." Her cat plopped down by her feet and purred loudly. "Marmalade agrees too."

"I'm not certain how I shall keep my hands off you over the days, weeks, and months to come, but I shall." Lightly, he stroked one finger down her neck before trailing over a small raspberry mole along the upper swells of her breasts where her pulse beat fiercely hard. He kissed the spot, his lips warm and his breath hot. "This pretty mole," he murmured. "I now dream of finding more just like it on your body, and kissing each and every one. Please tell me there are others."

"Y-Yes." She barely got the word out. "There is another on my belly, one on my right hip, and one on my, ah, inner thigh."

"How perfect." Grinning, he spread one hand over her belly, then smoothed over her right hip, heat radiating out from his scorching touch, although his hand didn't remain on her hip for long. He swept downward and pressed between her skirted legs, his smile turning dangerously dark. "The inner thigh of your left or right leg?"

"Right," she whispered raggedly. "We only have five minutes, of which they must almost be up."

"In the future, you'll need a chaperone when we're together, at all times. Marmalade will not do." He groaned as he stroked her inner thighs, her cat's purr getting louder. "I need to kiss you, Rosamonde."

"Oh, Richard, please do." She clutched his shoulders and held on tight.

"I adore it when you say my name with such breathlessness." He thrust his hips against her hips and his mouth met hers in a hungry kiss that had her gripping the lapels of his royal blue riding jacket and clawing to get even closer to him.

A knock rattled the door. "Is all well in there?" Avery called out.

"One moment." Winterly released her before stepping swiftly away and opening the drapes. Sunshine flared into the room and he muttered, "Come in, my friend."

She fussed with her hair, not that it was mussed thankfully, her hat still atop her head. She then tidied her skirts and the hem of her riding jacket, just as Avery stepped inside. Her brother scooped the missive she'd received from Roth from the side table.

With it in hand, he offered it to her. "No more secrets, dear sister. Read this letter to us both. Whatever Roth has to say to you, he must say to us as well."

"Of course." Composed again, or as much as she could be after being left alone with Winterly for five minutes, she slid her finger under the red wax seal holding Roth's insignia and opened the folded missive. She cleared her throat and read the words contained.

"Lady Rosamonde,
I won't be able to return to Hillhurst Hall until later this evening. I would be honored if you would join me for a

ride tomorrow morning. Be ready at ten.
    Regards,
    Roth."

Brow raised, she eyed Winterly who now stared outside, his jaw tight and his whitened knuckles pressed into the wooden windowsill. "I will, of course, decline his invitation," she murmured.

A low growl rumbled from her earl as he tipped his narrowed gaze at her. "I don't want him anywhere near you while Avery and I are away. You will invent an illness, a rather long-standing one."

"I already feel an ache of the head coming on." With trembling fingers, she refolded the note. "I'm certain it shall be pounding away before too long. I'm rather susceptible to megrims and require a darkened room with no noise permitted. The ache which throbs on one side of my head lasts for days and days. I'm often violently ill and suffer from intense dizziness too."

"That sounds positively, horribly, undeniably perfect." Winterly blew her a kiss. "Stay safe."

"I will." She blew him a kiss back. "Stay safe yourself."

"I'll escort you to your chamber so you can rest." Her brother slipped the missive from her fingers and pocketed it. "I'll send a response to Roth on your behalf, informing him that you are unwell and can't possibly agree to a ride, or even seeing him until you are on the mend."

"Thank you." She would do everything in her power to ensure she escaped Roth's company until Winterly and her brother returned from London, although she didn't doubt it would be a difficult feat to manage considering the upcoming events of the week and the fact that Winterly and her brother would be gone for nigh on two weeks.

She'd manage it though. Somehow she would.

Chapter 8

Following Rosamonde's retreat to her chamber to rest, Winterly joined in the hunt with Avery. It had been difficult to keep his attention focused on the hunt and as soon as he'd been able to break away from the main group of riders, he'd returned to the hall and sent Rosamonde a note, that he would collect her as soon as night fell and the skies had darkened. He had much to do in the meantime. He'd ordered his valet to remove all markings from his carriage, then he'd instructed his driver to await him at the end of the driveway half an hour after night had fallen, the lamp extinguished, with no one to learn of his coming departure.

Both his valet and driver would never speak of what was to unfold this night and they were loyal to him, having both served him and his father before him. He also required two witnesses for the ceremony, which would be taken care of by his two men. Their marriage must be legal and binding, so that he could ensure Roth couldn't make any claim on Rosamonde while he was away.

Certainly, no one else could learn of his elopement this night, not a single soul if he wished to keep any scandal to a bare minimum. Thank heavens Gretna Green was a mere three-hour ride from this estate so close to the Scottish Borders. They could travel there and return before dawn.

After excusing himself early from the evening meal in the dining room and wishing his mama and sister a good night, he strode to his chamber and donned a hooded cloak. Ducking through the shadows along the upper passageway to Rosamonde's rooms, he let out a long-held breath as he finally reached her chamber door. He raised a hand to knock then halted as another shadowed form eased out from a darkened nook a little farther along the corridor. Even with her black cloak covering her from head to toe and her fur-lined hood hiding her face, he had no doubt of exactly who awaited him. She drew back deeper into the niche where she'd hidden and he swept in beside her and caught the faint outline of a partially concealed door in the shadows.

On her toes, she whispered in his ear, "There is a stairwell behind me, which the servants use. It leads to both the kitchens and the cellar. From the cellar there is a short tunnel that runs underground before coming out in the rear gardens. No one in this house ever speaks of the tunnel to another and neither may you."

"My lips shall remain sealed." With his need to protect her a fierce beat in his blood, he opened the stairwell door, steered her through and closed the door behind him. A candle flickered within an iron wall sconce at the bend in the stairs below. "Show me the way."

"Of course, and mind the stairs. They might be made of stone but they're old and crumbly in a few places." Bunching the sides of her cloak tighter about her, she hurried downward.

Following her, he negotiated the cramped and dark space as he kept an eye both on her and his footing. He passed the lit candle on the landing then navigated the tight turn in the stairs. With his shoulders brushing the gritty stone walls, he had to stoop half over or else knock his head on the low beamed ceiling.

Rosamonde slowed next to a dark wooden door and touched the panels. Beyond the door the clang of pots and the chatter of the servants echoed back. "The kitchens are right through here, but we shall continue on downward."

"Then let's move, as quickly as possible." With a hand at the small of her back, he urged her to continue down the stairs, the air turning musty and stale as it clogged his throat. "How much farther?"

"We're almost there," she whispered as she too struggled to draw in a deep breath. "We're below the ground already."

"Allow me to take the lead. In case one of the servants is fetching wine or some other such thing from the cellar." Within the tight constraints of the stairwell, he shuffled past her, his chest brushing against her front, his hands on her shoulders as he held her steady on the step. Once he edged onto the lower landing, he halted before a paneled door and with a creak pushed it open an inch or two.

A candle burned in a holder opposite rows and rows of shelves holding hundreds and hundreds of wine bottles. He waited, one ear cocked as he listened for any possible noise. Not a sound echoed back, all remaining clear. Catching her gloved hand, her fingers so tiny within his, he tugged her inside the cellar and closed the door behind them. "Which way now?" he asked since two doors across the other side of the cellar appeared to lead in two separate directions.

"The corridor to the left leads to a large stone chamber where we store things which are small enough to carry down here. It's rather cluttered, to say the least, since nothing is ever disposed of. The passageway on the right leads to the tunnel which will take us to the rear gardens."

"We'll leave this candle here since I don't wish for anyone to catch sight of us by its light." He'd have to negotiate the tunnel in the dark. Gripping her fingers tighter, he led the way down the passageway to the right and when the candlelight from behind them no longer penetrated into the dark, he patted the sides of the tunnel to remain on course.

He traversed the depths of the tunnel, the cloying odor of dirt and grit strengthening the farther they walked, then nearly a hundred feet on the tunnel suddenly got smaller and even tighter, until he was forced onto his hands and knees. Crawling the remaining few feet wasn't an issue, not as a wave of fresh air blew in.

Taking care, he scrambled out the opening of the tunnel into the dark of the night, then reached back and aided Rosamonde to her feet. They'd emerged within the shadows of a clump of thick bushes with trees all around them. He took a moment to search their surroundings. A small creature scampered away in the undergrowth and a horse whinnied from near the stables. Expected noises.

Turning back to his lady, he kissed her fingertips. "I would have never known this entrance was here if I hadn't just come out of it."

"My ancestor who built Hillhurst Hall added the tunnel as an escape route. His second wife was the eldest daughter of a Scottish laird, and she insisted on the design addition, a rather clever one at that." She pushed her hood back and leaning saucily into him, wrapped her arms around his neck. A small trace of moonlight shimmered through the thick foliage overhead and sprinkled over her cheeks, her golden locks hidden by a red bonnet with satin ribbons tied underneath her chin. "We made it," she murmured with a stunning smile that melted his heart. "This might be the grandest adventure I've ever embarked on."

"We have only made it clear of the hall. We have a lot farther to travel this night."

"I know." A quick press of her lips to his cheek then she slid her hood back in place. "Cover your head, my lord. Your hood has slipped off."

"Kiss me properly and I shall."

"That was a proper kiss, quite suitable in fact." She giggled and tucked his hood back over his head for him. "What arrangements have you made from here? Do we travel by horseback or carriage?"

"My carriage awaits us at the end of the drive." Flicking a look in both directions, he ushered her through the trees toward the place where he'd instructed his valet and driver to await him.

Thankfully, the thin sliver of the moon aided them by disappearing behind clouds as they trekked down the driveway, their footsteps crunching the gravel. Right where he'd asked his men to wait, his valet appeared.

Peterson gave him a brief nod which meant all had gone well with ensuring his orders had been taken care of. His carriage awaited him, all insignia removed and his coachman up top. The carriage had been equipped with four of his finest and fastest bays, the horses stamping their hooves in eagerness to be away. After assisting Rosamonde inside, he clapped a hand on Peterson's shoulder. "Ensure Hocks makes all haste to Gretna Green. We must travel directly to the old blacksmith's shop and return before dawn."

"It is a rather fine night for travel, my lord." With a smile, his man bounded up top and sat next to Hocks.

"A rather fine night indeed." He stepped inside the carriage, closed the door, and removed his cloak just as Rosamonde had done. Peterson had ensured their comfort by lighting a brazier and warmth filled the cozy space. Rosamonde removed her bonnet next, along with her gloves and tucked her belongings underneath her seat. He flicked out his tails and settled himself on the lush burgundy squabs opposite his bride-to-be, his hands resting on his knees. "Are you comfortable?"

"Yes, I am." An excited spark flared in her eyes as she jiggled a little in her seat. She took a calming breath as she clasped her hands primly in her lap, her fingers pale against the skirts of her red woolen gown.

That gown was one she'd worn two years past at one of her mother's previous house parties, at an evening meal in which he'd been seated directly beside her. At one of her brothers' teasing jests, she'd laughed and sloshed a few drops of vivid red wine on herself. Discreetly handing her his handkerchief underneath the table, his fingers had brushed hers as she'd accepted the cloth. He'd kept that cloth, tucking it away in his pocket after she'd dabbed the wine away. He hadn't allowed his valet to wash it either but had stored it in the top drawer of his study desk at his townhouse. Whenever he opened that drawer, he'd reminisce about that night. All four of her brothers had been in attendance. West and William had arrived home on leave from their regiments, their fight across the channel against Napoleon a brutal one. Kipp, the earl's second-born son who resided in London, had returned home for the week to see his family. More memories surged, and he distinctly recalled the high neckline of the gown, which was currently buttoned all the way to her chin. That night so long ago, he'd wanted to loosen a few of those buttons, as he still did now. Clearing his throat, he met her gaze. "If you wish to rest for a spell and sleep for the journey, please do so."

"It isn't all that late yet." She straightened her shoulders, her eyes widening. "Oh, except you said you slept very little last night. If you're tired, then please don't allow me to hold you back from resting. I won't mind in the least."

"I am tired, but I'm also too enthused to sleep right now."

"So am I." She glanced toward the window, where Peterson had pulled the burgundy curtains shut in order to keep the warmth in and to provide them with privacy. She stared at the folds of swaying velvet before slowly returning her gaze to his, the twinkle in her eyes even more prominent as she smiled. "Richard, you are watching me rather intently."

"My apologies if I am." He wouldn't be able to watch her at all once he'd ridden for London in the morning, which caused his gut to tighten with immense frustration. "I'm already missing you, that's all."

"I'm right here with you."

"I'm projecting forward to tomorrow."

"Well, we must live in the moment, not in the future when we'll be parted." Daintily she crossed her slippered feet at her ankles, her red shoes matching her gown.

"That all sounds reasonable, except I'm suffering from the most uncomfortable feelings right now, of needing to keep you close since I won't be able to soon."

"That is a good need to have with your future wife."

"You don't mind that the vows we'll speak this night must be kept in secret?"

"I don't mind at all." Her eyebrows pinched together, a frown marring her forehead. "What if you and Avery can't secure the funds?"

"We will." He rose and sat beside her, took her hands in his and kissed her fingertips. "I can be rather determined when my mind is set."

"Avery is much the same."

"Yes, and between him and I, we'll ensure your father's debt to Roth is repaid." It was from sheer willpower alone that he withheld from lifting her from the squabs and settling her in his lap. His need to comfort her was an overwhelming emotion that tore at him deep inside.

With a soft sigh, she wriggled about to face him, her hands slipping free of his as she cupped his cheeks. Gently she smoothed along the skin underneath his eyes. "There are still dark circles here. Are you certain you don't wish to have a nap?"

"How about we compromise?"

"On napping?"

"Yes, let's lie down and if we fall asleep, then we fall asleep."

"All right." She nodded her agreement.

He turned the lamp inside the coach down, leaving it burning low before he returned to her and laid down on the bench. As she snuggled in front of him, he wrapped one arm around her waist, tucked his knees in behind her knees and released a long and contented sigh which fluttered her hair across her cheek. Naught had ever felt so wonderful, to have her ensconced so safely in his arms, her back to his chest and their bodies touching from their heads to their toes. His heart picked up in speed and thumped erratically fast. "Are you warm enough?"

"I'm delightfully warm, thank you." She wriggled around until she faced him and with a stunning, heart-melting smile, lifted her luscious lips. "Are you warm enough?"

"I am getting hotter by the second."

"We are well-suited, aren't we?"

"In every sense of the word." He trailed one hand up and down her arm, kissed the tip of her nose and drew her even closer. "Rosamonde," he whispered as he kissed her neck, so much need vibrating in his voice. "Within the course of a few days, you have turned my life upside down."

"You've done the same with me, but in the most wondrous way." She tucked her cheek against his chest. "It is lovely to cuddle like this, as if we truly are already husband and wife."

"It certainly is." He continued to hold her, until she succumbed to the blissful moment, her breathing slowly evening out. He relaxed fully too, the gentle rocking of the carriage and the warmth of the brazier so comforting, holding her in his arms even more so. He closed his eyes and slipped away into the restful dark.

Chapter 9

Their coach bumped over a hole in the road and Rosamonde knocked her head against Winterly's chin. She stretched on the coach's padded bench, absurdly happy as Winterly opened his eyes with a grunt. As he rubbed his eyes, she couldn't help but smile and kiss his chin where she'd bumped it. "Richard, this night, thus far, has been a divine adventure."

"It would be more divine if I were lying beside you in my bed, both of us as naked as the day we were born." He reached into his jacket pocket and removed his pocket watch. In the dim light of the lamp, he stared at the piece then repocketed it. "It's been three hours, so we can't be far from our destination. I'll take a look out the window. Up you get, my love."

She wrestled into a seated position, which allowed him room to sit as well.

Once he'd adjusted his tailed jacket, he swept the window curtain aside and peered out. A trace of moonlight flickered over the rippling waters of the River Esk which bordered the village of Gretna Green. She had traveled this road often over the years and knew it well. In the distance, lights shone from the stone cottages within the village, like a beacon of welcoming light guiding them through the dark of the night.

"We've made good time," he murmured.

"Yes, we certainly have."

"There's the blacksmith's shop." He motioned to the fork in the road where smoke curled into the air from the chimney and candles burned in the front latticed windows either side of the door, the shop surrounded by trees. "Except there is another coach outside the front door and a driver atop it. We'll need to wait our turn, but at least that means we won't have to awaken one of the anvil priests."

"Who does that coach belong to?" They pulled up alongside it in the wide circular driveway, the carriage holding beautiful scrollwork on each side but other than that no insignia graced the fine lines of the carriage.

"They seem to desire anonymity as we do." Winterly tapped the roof and called out, "Peterson, we'll wait until all is clear."

"Yes, my lord." An answer in the affirmative resounded from his valet.

"We'll ready ourselves though." In his tailed black jacket and fine black breeches, his white cravat knotted at his neck, he donned his cloak and eased the hood over his head.

She tidied her hair, slotted her bonnet in place and tied a bow underneath her chin with the silk ribbons. Gloves and cloak donned, her hood in place, she waited as

Winterly kept an eye on what happened out the window. A cloaked couple emerged from the front door and hurried down the steps. After they stepped into their carriage, Winterly allowed the curtain to sway back over the windowpane.

The clatter of wheels reverberated then tapered away.

Winterly opened the door and stepped down. He reached back, his gaze locked on hers as he extended his hand. She accepted his offer and he tightened his fingers around hers before drawing her down beside him and pressing a fleeting kiss across the top of her hooded head.

Sending a quick prayer skyward that all would go well, her vows with Winterly now mere minutes away from being spoken, she straightened her red woolen skirts underneath her cloak. She'd chosen this gown for a reason, not only for its warmth, but for the sweet memories attached to it. She touched the remnant stain of the wine drops she'd spilt on it a couple of years ago, which had never quite washed out.

"I remember," he whispered as he leaned into her ear. "I still have the handkerchief I loaned you to dab the wine drops away with. You look beautiful, and that small stain is the perfect accessory to your gown."

"Are we doing the right thing? If you wish to change your mind—"

"I'll never change my mind." He motioned to his men to await them both on the front step of the shop, then once they were completely alone, he cleared his throat, his expression turning rather serious. "What is your favorite color?"

"Oh goodness." She clasped a hand to her mouth.

"Blue, the same color as your eyes."

"I know you adore apple pie, but what's your favorite food?"

"It's actually raspberry tarts. What's your favorite color and food?" There were a hundred little important details she wished to know about him, which obviously he did too with her.

"It's now red, the same as your gown, and I enjoy anything savory or sweet. Apple pie is a particular favorite." He tucked her hand through his bent arm and guided her toward the shop, the light of the lamp near the door casting a soft, golden-yellow glow over the steps. "We will learn everything else there is to learn about each other in the weeks and months ahead."

"Yes, we will."

Winterly knocked on the door and it swung open.

A Scotsman dressed in tan buckskin breeches and a dark tunic, a dusty leather apron tied around his waist, filled the doorway. He took one look at their cloaked forms and beamed a toothy grin. "Welcome to ye. Ye two be the second couple who've arrived since nightfall. Come inside."

They followed the anvil priest into his workshop, the warmth from the fire burning from the hearth sweeping over her. Winterly halted before the blacksmith's anvil, which sat atop a central wide workbench. Various tools hung on the walls and hooks all around them.

She faced Winterly, with barely an inch between them, her slippered toes touching his booted feet as she looked into his beautiful eyes, which now shimmered with brilliant shades of pale blue and dark blue.

He cupped one of her cheeks before turning to the Scotsman who would soon marry them. "I'm Richard John Trentbury, the Earl of Winterly, and I wish to marry Lady Rosamonde Raven."

"Verra good, and what are the names of yer two witnesses, my lord?" The blacksmith placed a bible beside his anvil and metal hammer, set a piece of parchment next to it and wrote their names upon it. That document would be kept by Winterly should he ever need proof that their marriage had taken place on this day, at this time, and in this place.

"Mr. Henry Peterson and Mr. Horace Hocks, my valet and coachman, respectively."

"I'll record their names as well." The Scotsman dipped his quill into the ink bottle and scribbled their names down. Done, he lifted his bible and with it opened across his palms, eyed them both. "Do ye two come here of yer own free will?"

"I do." Winterly's answer came swift and firm.

"And ye, my lady?" the Scotsman asked her with one raised brow.

"I do." The man she was about to marry had saved her life six years ago and he was saving it again this night. Her hands shook, her heartbeat pounding. "I would never marry any other."

"I'll take that as your acceptance then." A beaming smile from the anvil priest as he clapped Winterly on the shoulder. "My lord, do ye take this fine young lass to be yer lawfully wedded wife?"

"Yes, I will." Winterly squeezed her hand encouragingly.

"Do ye," the blacksmith asked her, "take this man to be yer lawfully wedded husband?"

"I will."

"Aye, a fine marriage ye two will make. I'm certain of it." The blacksmith picked up his hammer and with a hearty voice, declared, "I hereby announce that Lady Rosamonde Raven and Richard John Trentbury, the Earl of Winterly, are hereby man and wife. In the name o' the Father, the Son, and the Holy Ghost, it shall be. I wish ye both a wonderful life together." He thumped his hammer down on the anvil, his tool of trade, the loud clanging of metal on metal ringing sharply about the room.

"We're married?" she asked the Scotsman to be absolutely sure.

"Aye, ye are." He chuckled as he laid his bible back down. "We Scotsmen dinnae believe in blathering on and on, although our women do have a penchant for doin' so, not that ye heard me say so." He wandered to his workbench and scooped a whisky bottle from the bench. Slugging a mouthful down, he gestured with one hand in a rolling motion to Winterly. "Ye may kiss yer bride, my lord."

"No." She stepped back from Winterly, her cheeks heating rapidly. She couldn't kiss him in front of all these men, not their first kiss as a married couple. Turning on her heel, she wished only to make her escape now that she'd spoken her vows and the deed was done.

Happiness should be the only emotion flaring through her in this moment, for she truly had wed her hero, but instead guilt had somehow weaved its way into her heart. She'd wed a man without her family present, for a very good reason of course, but still, she'd now spoken vows without them here to witness such a wondrous, life-changing moment, one in which they should all be celebrating together.

Instead, theirs would be a secret marriage, one she could never speak of to another.

Her guilt grew into a mountain of guilt as she hurried out the door. She swept down the steps and settled into the coach with Peterson's aid. Inside, she trembled from head to toe as she sat, then she waited for several long minutes until Winterly finally joined her with the parchment declaring them a married couple in his hand.

He removed his cloak, tucked the parchment roll safely away under his seat before tapping the roof and calling to his driver to make the return journey to Hillhurst Hall. Seated across from her, he crossed his arms as they bumped along the road. "Are you angry at me?"

"No. I'm angry at myself." She pushed her hood back, untied her bonnet and set it aside.

"Could you be more precise with your answer?"

She took several deep, calming breaths in an effort to maintain her emotions at a steady level. "I've acted rashly tonight, yet I'm glad I did. I'm also upset at this moment because I've denied my family the chance to wish me merry on my marriage, a marriage I can't even tell them about."

"You have always thought of your family first, and yourself second. It simply goes against your better judgement to do something that they might disagree with, although your father has already agreed we can marry."

"Yes, but with the proviso that the funds be found to

repay Roth first."

"I'll find them."

"How exactly?" She swept across to him, lowered to her knees at his feet and grasped his hands. "Please, tell me. I will fret otherwise."

"There are a few options. I've invested heavily in several marine trade ventures which have been rather profitable. I can pull some of those investment funds out, and what I'm short of, I'll ask a few of my friends to loan me. Does that help ease your mind a little?"

"Yes, although there is one other issue." Lowering her gaze, she bit on her lower lip, not sure how he would take her next words.

"Speak your mind, Rosamonde." He slid a finger under her chin and lifted her gaze back to his.

"Richard, I understand you don't wish to consummate our wedding vows, but I believe we should. Consummating them will ensure this marriage is as real as it could possibly be." She removed her gloves, plucking one gloved finger loose at a time, then she set her gloves aside and worked the top button of her woolen gown free.

"What are you doing?" He stiffened, his shoulders going rigidly tight.

"I'm feeling rather hot all of a sudden." She loosened the second and third button.

"You are not permitted to undress before me."

"I don't believe I asked your permission." She couldn't keep the teasing tone from her words.

"I am your husband and you must obey my orders."

"Which reminds me, aren't there certain duties that you, as my husband, must now honor? Particularly in regard to your performance of course." She kept going, working another button loose, then another until she reached her waist. She rose to her feet and shimmied her skirts down over her hips until they fell in a red pool at her feet. With her chemise still covering her adequately, she arched a brow. "Do you find me desirable?"

"That is a trick question. Of course I find you desirable, but there is a reason I don't wish to consummate our vows. It could be months until we actually wed. What if I got you with child?"

"Sometimes a married lady's first child comes early, but her second child is always on time. Have you heard that saying?" She settled herself on the squabs beside him, her knees touching his legs as she faced him, her hands clasped over his crossed arms.

"No."

"That saying was within a book I read recently to my mother, words which drew forth a giggle from her, although with no explanation for why. I pondered what those words might mean for two days before the truth behind them finally came to me. Avery arrived happy and healthy, seven months after my parents had wed—a first child coming early. The rest of us arrived on time."

"You wish to take that risk, of getting with child?" He uncrossed his arms then re-crossed them, his gaze dipping to the low neckline of her undergarment where the pretty trim of white lace sat flush against the upper swells of her breasts. Jerking his gaze back up, he muttered, "I, ah, you deserve to have a Season and I would be a lout if I didn't allow it. I want to court you properly, to visit the playhouses, to take rides in the park, walks along the

Serpentine."

"I'm not asking you to take away such delightful options, of allowing me to enjoy a Season, but I have attended various events here and there in the country, gatherings and country balls, soirees and dinner parties. I'm not one to engage in flirtation with gentlemen, nor do I understand the true art of seduction, but here I am, alone with you in your carriage, newly married but still untouched, dressed only in my chemise and…" She sighed as she played with the silk ribbons crisscrossing the front of her chemise, her movement attracting his narrowed gaze and a gulp which had his throat working. "Well, I feel as if there must be a way for you to ensure the chance I have of conceiving a child becomes limited. That would allow us to consummate our marriage and for any chance of falling pregnant to be lessened."

"There are ways, or methods as such," he admitted as he caught one of the ribbons at her neckline. He ran the silky length gently through his fingers until it slipped free and fluttered back to her chest.

"Please, Richard, speak of these ways to me. I need to know."

"Abstinence." Grinning, he leaned in and touched his lips to her forehead. "Which would be my preferred method."

"Yes, well I understand that." A mumble under her breath. He could be so infuriating at times. "Tell me more."

"There is the withdrawal method." He lifted her from the squabs and settled her on his lap.

"Oh, that sounds intriguing." She looped her arms around his neck, played her hands through his chestnut brown hair, the strands sliding so sensually through her fingers.

"It is a method by which the man withdraws his penis from the woman prior to releasing his seed, although it isn't foolproof." He caught one fluttering ribbon again and with a naughty wink, tugged the bow loose.

"Mmm, how interesting. Are there more options available?"

"We shouldn't be discussing this, but yes." He plucked at the top crossover of ribbon—with his teeth—which had her trembling in his arms.

"Do continue," she gasped with a panting breath.

"Well, there are sponges, or if a sponge isn't readily at hand, a plug of cloth can be used to capture the man's release deep inside a woman."

"Which method would you prefer to use, if we were to say…indulge in some conjugal activities?"

"Are you attempting to weaken my resolve, Lady Winterly?"

She couldn't help but smile as he addressed her by her new title.

"I certainly am, Lord Winterly."

He plucked another lacing free.

Chapter 10

"The withdrawal method would suit me the most," Winterly admitted, his wife's alluring silhouette outlined by the thin cloth of her chemise. "Rosamonde, if you do find yourself with child though, you must tell me, immediately, without any hesitation. Do we have an understanding?"

"Yes, Richard." She purred his name in such a sensual way, which had his cock getting very hard very quick.

Their coach bumped along the road, the curtains swaying over the window.

It was just them, only them, both tucked up in a cocoon of warmth.

He itched to remove her last layer of clothing and expose her body fully to his touch. He trailed his fingers along the bare skin of her inner wrist, and she released a delicious shudder that had his cock hardening even further.

"I adore being with you." She stared into his eyes, the blue-green depths of hers darkening with desire. "I don't want to resist these new emotions surging through me. I want your mouth on mine, your fingers on me below, and for our marriage to be passionate and fulfilling for us both. It is important to me that I provide you with as much comfort and support as I can, through good times and bad.

"That is the kind of marriage I desire as well, to provide you with the same." Gently cupping the back of her head, he drew her mouth to his and kissed her, tasting her enchanting sweetness. So good. She was his, the woman he'd made his wife, his countess and the new Lady Winterly.

He would bed her in his coach, but he'd do so with the utmost care for her virgin state, or at least he would attempt to do so. He would draw out her pleasure and safely tuck away every memory they made on their return trip home, then he would hold onto those treasured memories during the long days he'd soon be parted from her.

She tipped her head to the side, her lids lowering, her gaze lost to him for a few precious seconds. No, he needed to see her eyes. Just as he was about to ask her to look at him, she wet her bottom lip, her tongue darting out in an achingly nervous gesture. He wanted to nibble on her bottom lip, to see it swollen with fullness and know he'd caused it to become so plump and red.

Then her nervousness suddenly disappeared as she loosened the pins from her hair, slowly and deliberately. Long golden locks tumbled down her back in waves of silken glory.

His new wife was so exquisite to behold, her heart so giving, her lushly curved body made for the carnal pleasures he intended on indulging them both in.

"Do you want me, Richard?"

"I'm not certain how I've lived without you until this moment in time." He intended on showing her exactly how much he wanted her this night. Raw and desperate need swept through him like an avalanche. "I would like to be wicked with you in this carriage. Will you be wicked with me?"

"There is no one I would wish to be wicked with, other than you." A whimper escaped her throat. "I feel so hot."

"So do I." Heat pulsed through him, his cock throbbing as he slid his hand under the hem of her undergarment and cupped her mound with incredibly fierce possessiveness. It had been a long time since he'd last touched a woman in such an intimate way, two years to be exact, a time which coincided with when he'd rescued her and her kitten from a tree. Of late, he'd had to take his own cock in hand and pump himself until he'd released any sexual tension building within him. Now, he no longer had to. He lowered his mouth to the small raspberry mole on the upper swells of her breasts, flicked his tongue over the delicious spot and smiled as she moaned and arched her back. His cock wept to get closer to her. Gads, he hadn't been this eager for a coupling since the first time he'd been with a woman. Sixteen, he'd been at the time, imbibing on enough liquor to give him courage as he'd fumbled about with a maid from the local tavern.

Rosamonde batted her lashes, the yearning look in her eyes making his heart jerk. She'd spoken the truth from her heart, that she wished for this joining and as he kissed her, she met him with fervent need, her mouth voluptuously soft as she seduced him with tender nips and licks.

A touch of amusement radiated through him, that

she'd had to convince him of this path. Slowly, gently, he smoothed his thumb over her nub below, and she wriggled her bottom in his lap and spread her legs wider. He kissed her, hard and deep, the taste of her mouth so sweetly intoxicating. It wouldn't take long at all for him to get completely drunk on the taste of her, as well as completely greedy and overzealous for whatever she would offer him in the future.

There was her and only her.

Panting, he pulled back an inch and she smiled and began loosening his cravat, her eyes all dreamy and heavily lidded. No hesitation on her part, any nervousness of before now gone, and she surely didn't appear as if she wished to change her mind. He certainly had no intention of giving her the chance any longer, not now he'd committed to this new pathway for them both.

As soon as she had removed his cravat and allowed the white fabric to slide from her fingers onto the squabs, he pressed one finger deep inside her then caught her shuddering moan with his mouth. "My wife, you are so beautiful."

"I am also wearing far less clothing than you." Her cheeks flamed a rosy red.

"I'd rather you be completely nude." A dark craving for more heated his blood and he lifted her from his lap and laid her on the squabs. After gently plucking her slippers from her feet, he set her footwear on the floor and slid the hem of her chemise up her long legs, past her delicate ankles, over her slim calves and shapely thighs. Pressing one knee between her knees, he spread her legs wider and caught his breath when he found the small raspberry mole along the inner thigh of her right leg. Head dipped, he licked the mole and she grasped his shoulders, her nails digging in deep.

"Richard," she whispered. "That feels rather illicit."

"No part of your body will remain forbidden to me." He pushed her hem higher, uncovering a thatch of golden curls covering her mound. Breathing in her ravishing scent, he couldn't halt his need to take her fully and completely. Hell's teeth, everything about his seductive bride called to him, as if she had always held a piece of his heart and he'd been waiting for this time in his life when he could finally claim her. He was damned lucky she hadn't been stolen away from him by another man over the last few years. No other could steal her away from him now either, not since he'd made her his.

"What are you thinking that has that suddenly possessive look in your eyes?" She released his shoulders and braced her hands on the squabs either side of her, her palms flattened against the plush burgundy seat coverings.

"I'm an idiot for not asking your father for your hand in marriage sooner. I haven't even lain with another woman since the day I rescued you and your kitten from the tree."

"In truth, I've longed for children this past year or two, to start a family of my own. That desire stirred within me the day you rescued me and my kitten." She licked her lips as she smiled at him. "You've now come to my rescue a second time and there is only you."

"You're all I could ever hope for in a wife. You're dedicated to your family, lively and loving, steadfast and loyal. You are my match in every way, Rosamonde, and now I don't intend to allow even one inch of your body to go untouched tonight, not by my hands or my tongue. I will know all of you before we reach Hillhurst Hall." He wriggled her chemise higher and she lifted enough to aid him as he exposed her hips and another tantalizing raspberry mole. He swiped his tongue over it before peeling her undergarment higher, over her breasts, her nipples all peachy-pink and hard. His cock pushed against the waistband of his breeches, the head escaping and poking out. "Arms up, my wife."

Even though she was inexperienced and still blushing, she lifted her arms and he swept her chemise over her head. He dropped her chemise on the floor, all of her now exposed to his hungry gaze. His heart stuttered in his chest, then suddenly started pounding again.

"You are the most beautiful woman I've ever seen." Under the flickering light of the lamp, her creamy skin held a soft glow that beckoned and he tentatively touched one finger to her neck and trailed down between the valley of her breasts. As she moaned and arched into his touch, thrusting her breasts out farther, he accepted the offering of her body and cupped their fullness. He licked one nipple then the other, then returned to the first and suckled it deep inside his mouth.

"Oh my." She whimpered, her need for his touch clear to see.

"I'm not sure I can go as slowly as you require this first time." He unbuttoned the flap of his breeches and gripped his cock.

She gasped, the heated look in her eyes capturing his gaze. Tentatively, she reached out one hand and touched the head. She swirled one finger along the slit, her brows lifting as she caught the drop of his essence on the tip. With great curiosity flaring on her face, she brought her fingertip to her lips and gazed at him. "Tonight you've changed the course of my future. I no longer have to fear the Marquess of Roth, not when I secretly carry your name."

"I will never let him have you." He couldn't deny the depth of their connection, how fiercely it now roared to glorious life within him. She was his best friend's little sister, but more than that, she was now his wife.

"Richard?" Between them, she reached and gently cupped his balls with one hand and wrapped her other hand around his shaft, her actions scattering any of his remaining good intentions. "I am yours, and you are mine. Join us together as one."

"Yes, I'll always be yours." He leaned over her, captured her mouth and sucked her tongue between his lips. He kissed her and she moaned into his mouth, her grip tightening on his cock. Her touch was exquisite, as if she were attuned to him and understood exactly where he ached for her the most. His cock hardened and lengthened further, the shaft pulsing with a throb from root to tip that signaled he was running out of time.

Except he needed to aid her in finding her own pleasure first, which currently seemed like an impossible mission when he wished to explode. Although it was a mission he intended to accept and see to fulfillment.

Chapter 11

Rosamonde lost her sweet grip on Winterly's cock as he reared back onto his knees between her spread legs and swept his burning gaze over her body. She should be nervous about what was about to unfold, but she'd managed to set that emotion aside not long after it had arisen. Winterly was her childhood hero, a man who would never intentionally bring her any harm. From the moment he'd returned to Hillhurst Hall, he'd been intent on changing the course of her future. He'd detested the thought of her being wed to Lord Roth, and he'd become determined in his pursuit of her.

"What is going through that beautiful mind of yours?" Winterly kept his gaze locked with hers, his hands smoothing up and down her legs as he knelt between them, the tails of his black jacket flaring out behind him, his fine black breeches molded to his legs.

"Amazement that we're together, gratitude for the many ways in which we came to arrive at this point in time, and immense wonder that you are still dressed while I am utterly and completely nude." Their carriage bumped along the road in the dark of the night, the brazier still emitting warmth from the hot coals and the lamp providing a soft, gentle glow which cast his face in a sensual light.

"Then I'd best dispatch of my clothing." He unbuttoned his jacket and shrugged out of it, his white shirt impeccably pressed underneath.

She desperately wished to tug his shirt off him too, to have his bare chest pressed against her breasts. She opened her mouth to insist he continue disrobing, but closed it again as he suddenly lowered his gaze to her folds below and licked his lips. What on earth could be going through his mind to cause that kind of look? A devilish glimmer flickered in his eyes, then he bent his head. Surely, he wasn't going to—

He licked her slit and she lost her breath.

"Oh my." Eyes squeezed shut and her back arched, she twisted on the squabs as he teased her folds with hungry flicks of his tongue. Each of his swipes caused liquid heat to flare in her core, one fiery bolt of pleasure after another rocking through her. "Richard, I feel too much."

"No, I want you feeling far more than this. Relax back and enjoy what I'm doing, my love." He licked her sensitive slit again and again, rolled his tongue over her nub until she whimpered for more. More, he gave her.

He sucked her nub in pulsing spurts and her legs collapsed to the sides of the seat as she lost all ability to control her body. A mountain arose before her, one she began climbing. Higher and higher, she ascended until she held firm to the peak at the top. He drew back a touch and blew warm air over her folds, pushed two fingers deep inside her and swirled them about in a scissoring motion. She teetered on that edge, wishing to soar yet also wishing to hold onto this exquisite moment for as long as she could. As he added a third finger, she panted roughly, her moans escaping her as both pleasure and pain roared through her.

"Are you still comfortable?" He whispered the words as his cock saluted her high from the flap of his breeches, his shaft now even larger and longer than before, the plump head darkening to a deep raspberry color.

Not long ago, she'd swiped a bead of his essence from the flaring tip and a mixture of hungry and needy sensations had taken ahold of her. She'd wanted to do more than just wipe that bead away. She'd wanted to taste it, to take his shaft inside her mouth and suck on him, exactly as he'd just sucked on her.

"I'm asking," he continued, "because I need to prepare you fully for what's about to come, of my cock driving deep inside you."

"You are doing a wonderful job of preparing me." Still panting, she tried to stay in the present as his balls drew up tighter and higher into the thatch of dark curls at the base of his shaft. "I ache for you, Richard."

"That is the answer I seek." He licked her flesh again, in the most intimate way as he thrust three fingers in, his touch moving into a deep and delicious rhythm she completely adored. Every flick of his tongue and stroke of his fingers had her returning to that teetering peak at the top of the mountain, the sensations building higher and higher.

"Take me, please," she begged. Instinct roared to life and she wanted to let go, to take all that he offered and claim it, but not without him.

"Wait for me, Rosamonde." Hissing under his breath, he rubbed his cock along her slick folds, pushed against her thin barrier and thrust deep.

She gasped at the incredible fullness.

"Are you well?" he asked, holding still.

"Yes." Only a pinch of pain assailed her, his preparation having eased the way, his shaft buried as deep as it could go. "This feels so right."

"It is pure ecstasy." Hands planted on the squabs either side of her head, he eased out then slowly pushed all the way back in again. "I'll try to go easy. Hold onto me."

She clutched his backside, her folds getting wetter as he rocked so sublimely inside her. Covering her mouth with his, he kissed her until she arched into his body, then his kisses turned voraciously hungry as he picked up his speed and pounded into her. Moaning helplessly, she hooked her legs around his hips as he grinded into her. Gripping fistfuls of the back of his shirt, she held on and three strokes later, relentless waves of pleasure swarmed her. She came apart with a heartfelt cry, while he pulled out and left her bereft as he wrapped his handkerchief around himself and grunted as he came into the cloth. "Come back to me," she pleaded.

"I will." He tossed the cloth aside and pushed back inside her, his shaft not as rigid as before but she still basked in his return nonetheless, her inner channel continuing to throb and squeeze him.

"You feel incredible around me," he murmured in her ear. "You are my secret bride, whom from this day forth will be pleasured often at my hand, at every possible opportunity afforded to me. Never will I let you go again."

"Yes, I'm your secret bride," she whispered against his lips as he kissed her again.

She would never let him go either, not now she'd partaken of the wonders of their marriage bed, or as close to a marriage bed as she could currently hope for.

***

The ride back to Hillhurst Hall passed by in the blink of an eye for Rosamonde.

Winterly had fixed his clothing, while she'd wiped a smear of blood from her inner thighs with Winterly's handkerchief. Her new husband had then aided her in donning her chemise and buttoning her red traveling gown before he'd settled her in his lap. With her head resting on his broad shoulder, she'd dozed off and on, her body so languid and replete with pleasure she hadn't been able to remain fully awake.

"We're here," he murmured in her ear as he allowed the curtain to sway back into place after peering out the window.

"What is your plan now?" She stretched and yawned.

"It's still dark outside, although dawn won't be far away." He lifted her from his lap and rapped on the ceiling. "Halt at the end of the driveway," he commanded his driver.

The carriage slowed and rocked to a halt.

Winterly held out her cloak and she stood and pressed her hands against his chest as he swung the heavy folds over her shoulders and secured it at her neck. He looked into her eyes as he lifted her fur-lined hood over her head. "We shall return to the hall the same way we left, by way of the cellar tunnel."

She nodded in agreement, then pocketed her bonnet and gloves as he swung his cloak over his shoulders and tugged his hood over his head.

Once he opened the door and aided her to the gravelly ground outside, she scanned their surroundings. Darkness still clung to the night sky, stars glittering here and there with a small sliver of the moon shining through a light layer of night cloud. A smidgeon of paler blue sky hazed the far horizon where the sun would soon rise.

The hoot of an owl broke the stillness as Winterly left her side and spoke to his valet and coachman. Done with the instructions he'd issued to them, he returned to her, wrapped his warm fingers around her fingers and guided her up the driveway. They followed the darkened line of the driveway trees until the silhouette of the hall rose out of the dark. Candles burned in the front windows near the doors, but all the other windows remained shrouded in darkness.

"Come with me." Winterly led her through the rambling gardens, weaving through the trees toward the place where the tunnel entrance lay. In front of the scrub, he lifted the greenery aside and gestured for her to go first.

On her hands and knees, she crawled through the gap and negotiated the tight space until she was able to push to her feet as the tunnel ceiling rose higher. The cloying odor of dirt and grit strengthened the farther she traversed the darkened recesses of the underground passageway, Winterly close at her heels. Another hundred feet along, shadowy light flickered up ahead.

"Allow me to go first." Winterly held her steady by the

shoulders as he eased past her, then he continued on and she kept pace one step behind him.

Up ahead, a candle burned in a holder, its light shimmering over shelved rows holding her Father's wine collection.

Winterly stepped up to the door, waited with one ear pressed to the paneled wood and listened for any possible noise in the servants' stairwell. He tipped his gaze back toward her. "I can't hear even a snicker of noise."

"That is good. All must remain clear." She stepped up to him and cupped his warm cheeks, her heart overflowing with love for him. "I wouldn't wish for us to get caught together after we've taken such care thus far."

"I agree. We should return to our chambers separately so as not to be discovered with each other." He searched her gaze, a frown furrowing his brow. "I instructed my coachman to be ready to depart for London in a few hours. The horses need to be fed and to have a little time to rest, although the sooner Avery and I are away, the better. Before I leave though, I need your promise. You aren't to speak of our elopement to anyone, not to your family or mine, not to a living soul. It must remain a secret."

"I promise." She crossed her heart. "I'll take all care."

"You'll do more than that, Rosamonde." He searched her gaze. "Keep your maid close at all times. You must never allow Roth the chance to have a moment alone with you. Use the farce of having megrims for as long as you possibly can, then invent something else if need be."

"May I see you and Avery off at the front door?"

"It would be best if you didn't." He cleared his throat, his gaze narrowing with clear determination. "I've learnt tonight that I have very little restraint when it comes to you. Even now I wish to toss your skirts up and have my wicked way with you. Which cannot happen. Go straight up the stairs to your chamber, and keep to the shadows. Don't allow anyone to see you enter your room. That's an order."

"Yes, my lord." She wished to make things as easy as possible for him, so she obeyed, sneaking through the door and hurrying upstairs. No looking back. She would likely falter in her step otherwise. Hands brushing the gritty stone walls, she kept alert as she passed the flickering candlelight glowing from the wall sconce up ahead. Broken cobwebs fluttered and she swept one aside and ascended the last flight of stairs.

At the top, she slipped through the door and waited in the shadows of the niche.

No noise filtered through to her, so she ducked her head out and checked both ends of the passageway. All remained clear, her chamber door only a few feet away.

Keeping her hood over her head, she stole along the carpeted runner, opened her door and closed it swiftly behind her. With her back pressed to the coolness of the wood, she remained perfectly still. As she'd expected her chamber was cloaked in darkness, her drapes drawn across the square-cut windows and her fire unlit, exactly as she'd left her chamber last night, but something was wrong. Very wrong.

Chills rippled down her spine.

Her instincts screamed for her to run.

"About time you surfaced." The rap of a cane on the wooden floorboards had her searching the darkened corner near her armchair. A man's shadowy figure emerged from the dark, the whites of his eyes glowing and the scent of pipe-smoke assailing her senses. A cobweb clung to the collar of his fine gray jacket.

"W-what are you doing in my chamber? How did you get in here?"

"I didn't care for the missive your brother sent to me in response to my request that you join me for an outing. Your so-called megrim seemed to have come upon you at a rather convenient time, so I returned swiftly here last eve to my chamber down the passageway. I had intended to ask your maid about your health, but before I could, I spied two people in hooded cloaks disappearing down the servants' stairwell. When I ventured down there myself, I found no one else below-stairs other than the servants in the kitchens." His gray, flinty eyes narrowed. "I returned upstairs and knocked upon your door. To my surprise, I found no trace of you."

"I have been busy, that is all."

"I've been awaiting your return, and low and behold here you are wearing a hooded cloak. Whom did you sneak away with last night, Lady Rosamonde?"

"This is my home and I won't be questioned by you within it."

"If you were one of the two cloaked forms, then who was the other? Lord Winterly perhaps?" Moving a step closer, he stabbed his cane into the floor by her foot. "He seems to have taken a rather intense interest in you since his arrival."

"He is my brother's best friend and I've known him a long time."

"You are my future bride, not his."

She stiffened.

"Tell me," he snapped, spittle flying from the grim slash of his lips. "What have you been doing with Winterly for the past eight hours? If you have taken him as your lover, I shall thrash you to within an inch of your life."

"I would never take a man to my bed, not unless I'd wed him." She wouldn't allow Roth to darken Winterly's honorable character, although she also couldn't speak the truth about her elopement. She'd promised Winterly she wouldn't tell a living soul, and she would honor his request.

"Damn you." He backhanded her and she hit the wall, blood spurting from a split in her lip, her cheek throbbing. In her face, he bit out, "I have no intention of losing you to another man, just as I lost your mother. I shall request a special license so we can be wed in three days' time. Until then, you will come with me."

"You can't take me from my home."

"I'll leave a note here in your chamber for your parents, then I will find a priest who will marry us and once we've spoken our vows, I'll ensure the earl and countess are made aware that we are man and wife. "

"No, please, I beg—"

He shoved her into the wall and she hit her head with a mighty *thunk*. She swayed and the room spun.

"Restrain her, Hobbs." Roth stepped back and crossed to her writing desk.

Another shadowy figure stepped clear of the far corner. A second intruder. The man stormed toward her and before she could scream, he stuffed a foul-smelling cloth over her nose. The abrasive stench clogged her throat and black dots danced in front of her eyes. She gagged, her legs dropping out from under her.

Hobbs heaved her up and her belly thumped into his rock hard shoulder. Belladonna. A sedative. It laced the cloth with its acrid scent. She tried to open her mouth and yell for help, only all went dark and she sank into complete and utter oblivion.

Chapter 12

A few hours later and agonized at having to leave so soon, Winterly stood at his chamber window as Peterson finished packing his belongings for the trip to London. Gray morning clouds cast a heavy pall over the sky, his current mood just as despairingly dreary. Being deprived of his bride for the next two weeks that he'd be away wouldn't be easy. How he would manage the months during their coming courtship where he'd be forced to remain apart from her for days and weeks on end, would be damned difficult.

"Let's break our fast before we leave, shall we?" Avery strode into his room wearing buff breeches and a beige jacket and white neckcloth. His lifelong friend frowned as he eyed him from head to toe. "Is everything all right? You appear out of sorts."

Tugging on the hem of his blue silk waistcoat, the collar of his matching jacket flicked high over his impeccably tied black cravat, he offered Avery a smile which he dredged up from somewhere deep within him. "All is well, my friend, I assure you. Shall we break our fast in the dining room?"

"Yes, I caught the mouthwatering scent of bacon, sausages, and fresh bread wafting up the stairs as I made my way to your chamber."

"You truly do have a superb talent at dissecting scents from a great distance."

"Well, thank you. It is a skill I learned at a very young age and has always seen me in good stead." Beaming, Avery clapped him on the shoulder and urged him out his door.

Trotting downstairs, he silently counseled himself with each step he took, as he'd done since his return from Gretna Green. It was his duty to consider his wife's needs above his own, her greatest need that of having more time here at Hillhurst Hall with her mother. He would see that done, no matter if it killed him.

In the dining room he pulled out a navy padded chair and sat at the table which easily seated a dozen. A footman stood near the door, although he and Avery appeared to be the only two who had yet arisen even though it was half past ten.

He laid a napkin over his lap and partook of a hearty breakfast of bacon and eggs, sausages and fried tomatoes, followed by fresh bread rolls and a cup of steaming hot chocolate poured by a maid who arrived to attend them. As he ate, Avery read to him from the newspaper then showed him a caricature drawn of a couple amongst the *ton* who were currently causing the most intense scandal. The daughter of a duke had recently wed a viscount, the two of them arguing rather loudly during a gathering at Almack's, in which the viscount had ended the argument by scooping his lady up and stalking from the building with her in his arms. The caricature showed the gloriously-gowned lady with cheeks puffed out and steam rising from her head, while her newly wedded husband smirked with great delight.

"Good morning, Avery, Winterly." Hillhurst walked into the room pushing Lady Hillhurst in her wheeled chair, the lady's day gown a soft shade of pale pink, her golden hair holding a few streaks of gray, her locks twisted into an elegant chignon with a sprig of dainty white flowers tucked in the top. The liveried footman removed a chair next to the earl's chair at the head of the table where her ladyship usually sat.

"Good morning to you too, Father, Mother." With a mischievous smile, Avery added a splash of brandy to his hot chocolate from a flask. "Did you both sleep well?"

"Very well." Hillhurst tucked his wife's wheeled chair into place, dropped an affectionate kiss on the top of the countess's head and once assured of his lady's comfort, he took his seat. A maid attended them, serving breakfast foods and pouring both the earl and the countess hot drinks and once the maid had retreated back to the side table, the earl flicked a hand dismissing the servants completely from the room.

The footman closed the door quietly behind him and the maid.

Once they were alone, the earl glanced from him to Avery and back to him. "Winterly, my wife and I both wished to join you and my son to break our fast before the two of you departed for London."

Lady Hillhurst pressed a hand to her chest, her blue-green eyes the exact same shade as Rosamonde's. "My lord, my husband and I are beholden to you."

He held up a hand. "I'm certain it is I who is beholden to you."

"No." A firm shake of her head. "I know my daughter well and she agreed to marry Lord Roth because that was what her father had asked of her. She understands her duty to her family, but I pray you will be successful in your current endeavor taking you and Avery away from Hillhurst Hall this day. I truly wish only to see her happy, and that happiness will be certain if she is permitted to wed you. Rosamonde has always been extremely fond of you." The countess smiled then cleared her throat, her gaze lowering to the lacy white tablecloth then back to him. "Well, more than fond. One could almost say she's been smitten with you since you rescued her and me from those awful highwaymen six years ago. I also spoke to Rosamonde yesterday afternoon, while she was sequestered in her bedchamber, and my daughter's worry was clear to see. She is hopeful that you and Avery will be successful, but in the meantime, until your return, I shall do my utmost to ensure Lord Roth is aware she is unwell and unable to converse with him. Her father and I will do our best to delay the marquess in his endeavor to speak vows with her at the end of the month. We will invent whatever necessary illnesses are needed, so do not fear that we will allow her to leave this house before you and Avery return."

"Thank you. Your words greatly reassure me. Certainly those within the peerage rarely wed in order to accommodate the whimseys of our hearts, but in truth I am extremely fond of your daughter too, and will miss her terribly while I'm away. I give you my word I will secure the funds needed so you are no longer beholden to Roth."

"We will return the payment on those funds within five years," Hillhurst stated with firm authority. "I would much rather be in debt to you, Winterly, than I ever would with Roth. There is also the matter of Rosamonde's dowry which will be paid directly to her future husband upon her marriage taking place. Those are funds which remain untouched. Twenty thousand pounds in full."

Funds to use as he pleased, but which he intended to offset against Hillhurst's debt to him. His papa had taught him that family came first and that should one of them need aid, then they offered that aid. "Then if you will allow, I would prefer to reduce your debt by the same figure." He reached out a hand toward Hillhurst. "Do I have your agreement?"

"You are a credit to your papa, Winterly. May he rest in peace." Hillhurst shook his offered hand. "He was a wise man, loyal beyond measure, with deep affection for his family. I will accept your gracious offer and ask that you make all haste to London, then return as swiftly as possible."

"That is my intention." He wouldn't let either Rosamonde or her family down.

"Before you leave though, there is more I need to speak to you and Avery about." Hillhurst leaned forward, his gaze intent. "I'm referring to both my past, and my wife's past...with, ah, Roth."

"James, no." Lady Hillhurst gripped her husband's

arm.

"Elizabeth, Winterly needs to know the full truth, and so does Avery. We are still withholding information from them, information they need to know. It's time we came clean on everything." Hillhurst rubbed his wife's hand resting on his arm and when she sighed and nodded her head in acquiescence, the earl eyed him again. "My wife and I knew each other for years before we wed, but a few months before Elizabeth's debut Season, we became extremely close. I was enamored by her, and she with me. When I approached Elizabeth's father to ask for her hand in marriage, he wouldn't grant his approval. Her father had wished for her to marry the Marquess of Roth and had even entered into negotiations with him."

"That's who Mother was set to wed before you stole her away?" Avery's mouth gaped open.

"Yes, my son, and he told me quite bluntly that his daughter would never wed me, not since I was naught but the third son of an earl and Roth already titled following his father's passing. I was left with no choice but to steal my wife away even though a formal betrothal announcement had been agreed between her and the marquess. I kidnapped Elizabeth, who had no issue with being kidnapped, and thus we ran away to Gretna Green. That caused a great deal of strain between her and her parents for the first few months of our marriage. Then of course my elder two brothers passed away so soon afterward and I was suddenly overcome with becoming the new Earl of Hillhurst. It was a difficult time as I grieved for my lost family members, as well as stepping up and learning all that I needed to, in taking the reins of this estate and all it entailed. Since we had embroiled ourselves in a rather intense scandal at the time, due to our clandestine marriage, we'd also been shunned by those within our Society. My wife and I gladly redrew here to the hall, until a sufficient amount of time had passed, our scandal having been swept aside by the many other scandals that had followed ours."

"Sir, I would never allow a scandal to arise regarding Lady Rosamonde." No one would ever learn he'd already taken her as his wife, and hell, he wished he'd known about all of this before he'd stolen Rosamonde away to Gretna Green. Now, both mother and daughter had been betrothed to the same damned groom and carted away to the Scottish border by other men. "Is, ah, Rosamonde aware of what you've told me?" he asked Hillhurst.

"Yes. She overheard Roth and I arguing over the issue directly before the house party began." Elbows pressed to the tabletop, Hillhurst steepled his fingers together. "I humbly place my trust in you, Winterly, and you too, Avery, that this information doesn't get shared with anyone else."

"Of course it won't, Father. My lips are sealed." Avery nodded firmly, one corner of his lips suddenly cranking up. "Although, can I say, that I'm mightily glad you kidnapped Mother?"

"Yes, you can."

"I'm exceedingly glad your father kidnapped me too." Lady Hillhurst smiled so sweetly at her husband. "I do believe it is time for me to return to Society once all of this mess is sorted. I need to set my injury aside and live my life again, and after all the events of this past week, I now see that more clearly."

"You truly wish to visit London?" Hillhurst squeezed his wife's hand.

"Yes, provided you are with me. I don't want to be the one to hold our daughter back once she is wed to Winterly. She will feel great guilt if I remain here while she is enjoying herself in town."

"Agreed, and I'll be with you the entire time." A beaming grin from Hillhurst.

A knock broke their conversation and Hillhurst called out, "Come in."

A maid in a frilly white cap entered and closed the door behind her before hurrying around the table to the earl and his wife. With trembling fingers, she extended a note to Hillhurst.

"What do you have there, Mary?" Hillhurst accepted the note. "Speak up, girl."

"My lord, I found this note in Lady Rosamonde's bedchamber. My lady's bed hasn't been slept in, and I—I—" A tear trickled down her cheek, a sob tearing from her throat as she pulled a crumpled cloth with an acrid scent wafting from it from the depths of her apron pocket. "I found this too, in the servants' stairwell. It reeks of Belladonna."

The countess gasped, a hand fluttering over her mouth.

Avery reared back, his chair toppling over.

Winterly was struck numb, a loud buzz roaring away in his head.

Hillhurst ripped the seal on the note and scanned the letter. Darkness spread over his face as he read the words, then he snapped a look at the maid. "Search the entire house for my daughter. Ask the butler for his aid, but be warned, do not speak of what you've seen with anyone else."

"Yes, my lord." She dashed out the door and closed it behind her.

Hillhurst cleared his throat, his voice gritty and hard as he muttered, "This note is from Roth, addressed to me. I'll read it to you all." A deep breath from the earl. "Hillhurst, I have kidnapped your daughter, my forthcoming bride, just as you kidnapped Elizabeth and stole her from me all those years ago. I expect no recrimination for doing so, not when you have already agreed that I might wed the lady. I shall secure a special license and she and I will speak vows before a priest in three days' time. I shall ensure that you and your countess receive a letter following the confirmation of it. You are not permitted to raise a scandal over this issue, nor to visit Rothgale Manor until I expressly allow it. Should you attempt to interfere, then I'll ensure my wife never sets foot within Hillhurst Hall again."

"No." A heartfelt cry tore from the countess.

"Hell and damnation." Hillhurst ripped the note in two, strode to the fire and tossed the remnants of it into the glowing flames. Gripping the mantel over the hearth, the earl stared out the window overlooking the lawn.

Fury consumed Winterly and fisting his hands, he thumped the tabletop as he stood. The fine china rattled. No, he needed to corral his anger and remain calm. Riding to London was no longer on his agenda for the day, but riding to Rothgale Manor was. He had to rescue his lady and ensure Roth paid for his evil and atrocious behavior. Eyeing Hillhurst, he muttered, "Do you think he's truly taken her to Rothgale or could that just be a ruse?"

"We can't be sure until we search the manor, which we will, no matter what Roth has declared." Hillhurst gritted his teeth as he cast his gaze at Avery. "All care will be needed in infiltrating our neighbor's residence."

"Roth clearly has no idea of the lengths we would go to in ensuring Rosamonde's safety." Avery stormed the room from wall to wall.

"I believe he does, which is why he's abducted her." Hillhurst returned to his wife and kneeling next to her wheeled chair, rubbed her chilled hands between his. "Thankfully Roth is arrogant enough to believe we'd follow his decree, which of course we won't."

"We must find our daughter and bring her home." Tears pooled in the countess's eyes as she squeezed the cloth used against her daughter before tossing it aside. "He hurt her, and he must pay for doing so."

"Agreed, and to hell with whatever scandal comes. We must now think only of our daughter."

"We must also come up with a plan." Winterly had always prided himself on his abundance of patience, but at the moment his patience had been swallowed whole by his fear for Rosamonde. He also couldn't help but feel angry at himself since he should have walked her to her chamber and not sent her on ahead. If he had been with her, Roth wouldn't have been able to get his slimy hands on her. Clearing his throat of the thickness swelling it, he mumbled, "I propose Avery and I steal into Rothgale Manor, just the two of us. We must ascertain first if she is there. If she is, and we can sneak her safely out, then we'll do so. If not, then we'll return to the hall for further aid and storm the manor with as many men as we possibly can."

"That is an exceptional idea." Hillhurst rose from beside his wife, his gaze moving from Avery to Winterly. "Roth is a very private man and never opens his home, but while he was away in London one year, my wife and I visited his second wife for afternoon tea. There are three wings and over a hundred and fifty rooms."

"I'll never forget our visit to the manor that day." The countess squeezed her husband's hand where it rested on her shoulder, her gaze on Winterly and her son. "Lady Roth seemed rather frightened at our unexpected arrival, but she called for tea and we sat in her front drawing room. When she got called away by a servant to attend to an issue, she first asked her butler to show us to the gallery on the second floor. My husband and I wandered upstairs and viewed the portraits of the marquesses who had lived in years gone by. I was fascinated, being the artist that I am. The marchioness soon joined us and I learnt she was a vicar's daughter, her parents having not long passed away when she met Roth. She was most grateful to him, that he'd asked her to be his wife after he'd not long buried his first wife and his two young daughters from that union. The three of us spoke and enjoyed our afternoon together. Lady Roth mentioned that hers and her husband's chambers were located on the upper floor of the south wing. We didn't enter that wing, but my memory is very sharp when it comes to details. I can draw an adequate floorplan which will lead you to the upper gallery, which borders the south wing."

"I wonder why Roth rarely permits visitors to his manor?" Winterly stroked his jaw, that thought having always set him at unease. "He must be hiding something."

"All I can say is that Roth has always been that way," Hillhurst added. "Roth is very private when it comes to his home. I've simply never known him to be any different."

"You both must be exceedingly careful during your coming mission." The countess shifted a little in her wheeled chair before finding a comfortable position again. "It would be best if you waited until nightfall, so you could use the cover of darkness to shield your presence."

"That is exactly what we shall do, Mother." Avery walked around to the countess and pulled her wheeled chair from the table. He steered her toward the door with a glance over his shoulder. "It's time for the four of us to retire to Father's study so Mother might begin drawing the floorplan for us."

"Yes, let's do that." Winterly wholeheartedly agreed. He and Hillhurst followed the others, and as he trod down the passageway, he made a firm promise deep in his heart, to his wife. *I will find you, Rosamonde. I will never let you go.*

Chapter 13

Wave after wave of nausea crashed through Rosamonde, her belly churning. She shivered in the windowless bedchamber even though the blanket she'd wrapped around herself was thick enough to keep the chill in the air from seeping into her bones. She'd awoken from the Belladonna as Hobbs had carried her through the front door of Rothgale Manor, Roth marching only a few feet ahead, his hat under one arm and five bloodied fingernail scratches gracing the bald patch atop his head. She'd turned her own hand over and caught the dried blood coating the tips of her nails. When she'd scratched him, she had no idea. She must have done so while under the effects of the Belladonna, lashing out subconsciously.

Roth's portly butler had opened the door, then stood aside to allow them entry, the staff member not uttering a word. He hadn't even appeared surprised at seeing her, or that she was gagged, her hands bound in front of her. When Hobbs set her on her feet, her cloak dragged by the laces around her neck in a stranglehold, and her hair hung in a stringy, tangled mess, her breasts strangely aching.

Roth strode up the main stairwell, then halted halfway up and peered down at Hobbs with a frown. "Once the lady has bathed and changed, bring her to my chambers. Find my late wife's maid to attend her. What was the girl's name?"

"Mabel, my lord. She aids the housekeeper. I'll fetch her."

"Yes, yes, fetch Mabel after you've locked Lady Rosamonde in the marchioness's bedchamber." The marquess slid his gray, flinty gaze to her. "The bedchamber which shall be yours."

She glared at him in return, wanting to scream and shout, but the gag prevented her from doing anything more than muttering nonsense no one could decipher, let alone hear. Never would she give in without a fight though, not when she had no intention of becoming the next lady of this house. If it was within her power, she'd ensure there'd never be another Lady Roth who ever had to suffer such torture at his hands again. What his late three wives must have gone through during their short lives now seemed more than obvious. He was a tyrant, who must have kept them bound to this house which was why she'd never seen them.

The marquess smirked. "My lady, there is naught I enjoy more than seeing the fight in a lady's eyes slowly diminish and die a fast death. Soon enough you'll understand and accept your fate. I own you, which means I'll be permitted to punish you as I see fit, beating you to within an inch of your life if I so desire. I'd rather not do so of course, or at least not until you've given me a son. Until then I shall punish Mabel whenever you disappoint me. She has thick skin and is used to the beatings."

He was a devil dressed in fine clothing.

"Get on with you. Upstairs." Hobbs shoved her from behind and she'd stumbled forward.

While she'd trod up the stairs, she'd noted every inch of the pathway so she could easily find her way back out again when she finally escaped, which she would. Her stubbornness knew no bounds. After Hobbs had locked her inside the marchioness's chamber, only a lamp on the mantel over the unlit fireplace to provide light, he left with a gloating snicker. He was the devil incarnate number two, right after Roth.

Hours had passed before the door finally swung open again and a maid entered. She'd wanted to talk to the girl, but the gag still remained in her mouth. She had observed the maid instead. The girl had a terribly scared face, her pale eyes flickering warily toward her seated on a hard-backed chair next to the bed. The maid knelt at the hearth and set to work on lighting the fire. Before too long flames blazed and she added a log to the stack of burning wood.

Hobbs returned, opening the door wide for two barefoot lads who carried a wooden tub between them. They set the tub in front of the fire, their chins smeared with dirt and their breeches yellowed and torn at the knees. The lads returned within short order and filled the tub with pails of steaming water. One of the boys snuck a look at her under the oily fall of his dark fringe and got a kick up the backside from Hobbs for doing so.

"Out, Mabel." Hobbs pointed at the door and the maid

scurried out. "Wait in the passageway until I give you leave to enter again," he issued before closing the door. The man's dark beady eyes glinted in the firelight as he crossed to her, then gripping her chin, he eyed her bruised cheek. "You mustn't anger the master," he muttered. "My lord has never shied away from punishing his previous wives as he saw fit, and he'll do the same with you. Obey his orders and you won't have to suffer his wrath again as you've already done."

She mumbled through the cloth.

"If I remove your bindings you must promise me you won't scream or lash out. If you do, Mabel will be punished." He narrowed his gaze as he waited for her answer.

Since she couldn't escape from this hellhole until she'd had her restraints removed, she nodded her agreement. Patience. She'd need patience, to wait until just the right moment before making her escape. Whether that be an hour from now, two hours, or more. She would bide her time and choose the perfect moment.

He removed the bindings from around her mouth, plucked the gag free then worked the rope from her wrists.

She wet her dry lips and winced as her split lip opened again, the metallic taste of blood filling her mouth. Breathing deep, she firmed her resolve. "Roth can't force me to say marriage vows with him. No priest would allow such a thing."

"With enough blunt paid to the priest to keep his mouth shut, it won't matter whether you speak vows or not. You will be his wife in three days' time."

"And who exactly are you to say so?" She needed to

arm herself with as much knowledge as possible. "Are you Roth's servant, or one of his staff members?"

"I am his younger brother." He lifted his chin and stared down his nose at her.

"Roth doesn't have any brothers."

"I'm a by-blow from his father. The late Marquess of Roth had an affair with—well, with a fair number of the servants in this house. He favored me over the others though since I looked the most like him. I was schooled by a tutor right here at Rothgale. I'm also going to be the one to bed you, not my brother."

"Pardon?" Her ears rang. "Did you say—"

"You heard correctly."

"Why would Roth allow such a thing?"

"My brother, unfortunately, suffered an injury several years ago that left him without the ability to get his third wife with child. When he wed her ladyship, I lay with her, not my brother. Although Roth certainly participates where he can. He has always enjoyed using restraints on his wives, bringing about pain to ensure their full cooperation, sampling what he can when he does, and of course watching the final stages of the bedding."

"Are you quite serious?" She couldn't even imagine such debauchery.

"I'm simply warning you now that when Roth takes you to his bed tonight, I shall be there too, bringing you an equal amount of pain as well. There may be a little pleasure, if pain is your plaything." He tugged on the lapels of his austere gray jacket. "Just remember, should you not permit my touch, you'll be punished for it."

"That is scandalously, horrendously, despicably

wrong." Her vision blurred and when he snapped his fingers in front of her, she blinked to bring the room back into focus.

"I see I've distressed you with my words, but it is better you are told now so you might get used to the idea before the bedding. My master is eager for an heir and no one will set that desire aside." He paced to the door and rested one hand on the handle. "No one leaves Rothgale Manor alive, my lady, so it's best you get any thought of escape out of your head."

He opened the door and called out for Mabel to return. While he issued instructions to the maid who didn't appear any older than her, she snuck a look into the darkened passageway lit by a candle within a wall sconce across from her door. The flickering candlelight flared over the face of a guard standing tall in his position on duty.

The door closed with a clink as Hobbs left.

Trapped, and this time, not even by a key turning in the lock.

Shivering violently, she rubbed her chilled arms that even the warmth of the fire couldn't penetrate.

"This chamber is always rather chilly. I'll have you warm in a jiffy, my lady." Mabel added another log, then tipped rose oil into the tub and swished the water. "Do you need aid in undressing?"

"I do." She'd never be able to manage the tiny buttons down the front of her red woolen gown with her cold fingers. She rose from the hard-backed chair, the gray and black tartan blanket she'd wrapped herself in sliding to the floorboards.

Mabel scooped the blanket up and flapped it over the

bed. A dressing table sat against the wall with an oval mirror holding a crack across one corner, while a gray curtain hung in front of the ambry, the folds of it having collected dust in the creases.

Her maid fumbled with her buttons a little, two of her fingers rather stubby where the tips had been sliced away, her fingers having healed into a scarred mess. She didn't want to even ask how Mabel had come by the injury, or the terrible scarring on one side of her face, not when she already suspected it had occurred at Roth's evil hand. "What age are you, Mabel? And how long have you served in this manor?"

"I'm three and twenty, and I served the late Lady Roth in her parents' home as her maid before she wed his lordship six years past. I traveled with her here to Rothgale and remained by her side until her death." Done with the buttons, Mabel slipped the sleeves down her arms and tugged the gown past her hips to the floor. Mabel draw her chemise down her body too.

Once she'd stepped free of her clothing piled on the floor, she gasped at the tender pain in her breasts.

Mabel gasped too, her pale eyes going wide as her gaze alighted on her chest. "Damn that man," her maid muttered and clasped a hand to her mouth. "Oh, and please mind my language, my lady. At times, I have a wayward tongue that even the master of this house has struggled to tame. I can see your face is bruised, your lip split, but your breasts have been mauled. Do they hurt?"

"Mauled?" She quickly stepped in front of the cracked oval mirror and gasped at the mottled bruising darkening both of her breasts. Gently, she touched both mounds then her blackened cheek and sore lip. "I'm aware of how my face became bruised, but not my breasts."

"His lordship used Belladonna on my lady almost every day, to quieten her when she became agitated. When she was asleep under its influence, he would maul her breasts in this manner. That mauling caused her to be in constant pain."

"Why would he do such a thing? To exact such extreme punishment?"

"Because he is the devil himself, if you don't mind me saying." Mabel opened the top drawer of the dressing table and removed the cork from a wide-rimmed bottle.

"I don't mind you saying so at all, not when I'd already thought the same myself. I prefer the truth over lies. Thank you for being honest with me."

"Mistress, you'll get only the truth from me." Mabel dipped one finger into the bottle and smeared a creamy lotion over her cheek, then her breasts.

Her skin tingled, going a little numb. "That feels good," she murmured.

"The lotion helps to ease the bruising and the pain. Her ladyship applied it three times a day, every day, for each and every year she remained in this house. I recommend you do the same, and if you are too tender, then I shall do it for you."

Hot tears burned behind her eyes and scolded her cheeks as they flowed free. She wasn't crying for her own pain though, but the pain of the servants in this house who were innocent of any wrongdoing, who'd had to live under the marquess's roof. Sniffing, she gripped Mabel's hand. "Please, tell me how many servants in this house are good and kind as you are?"

"Myself and two of the household maids. The guards are all as evil as the master, Hobbs and the butler as well. The housekeeper, cook, and laundress all turn a blind eye to the goings on and are no good if you ask me."

"Give me the names of the two innocent maids."

"Young ones, they are. Thirteen and Fifteen. Ida and Bertha. Both bear fingers like myself, but their faces remain unscarred as yet. The master flogs as he sees fit and since I cared for my lady as well as I could, I sometimes got in the way of his raised fists." Mabel's eyes pooled with tears before she ducked her head and motioned to the bath. "Best you get in quick before the water cools."

Taking Mabel's advice, she stepped into the tub and sank down into the warm water. She took care to keep her breasts from getting wet so the lotion could continue numbing her flesh, but she washed her arms and legs and belly. "I've always bruised rather easily, unfortunately."

"I'll take care of you," Mabel promised in a gruff whisper as she glared at a connecting door along one wall.

"Is Roth's chamber through there?" She shivered as the water cooled.

"Yes, my lady." Mabel knelt at the edge of the tub and sloshed water over her hair. She gently cleaned and rinsed her locks then held out a drying cloth for her.

She rose, stepped clear of the tub, and allowed Mabel to wrap the cloth around her. Mabel left her side and foraged in the ambry, then returned with a shift and a plain blue day gown. She lifted her arms and the shift went over her head. Next the gown, which had short puffy-capped sleeves, a high waist and lacings at the front. The slightly musty folds swept down her hips and swished to her ankles. "I wish I could have helped your mistress," she whispered to Mabel.

"There would have been little you could do for her. She was trapped in this house and rarely permitted outdoors. On the very rare occasion when she traveled to the village, she had a guard ride with her."

"Before the marquess abducted me, he promised my father that I could visit my family as often as I pleased." Clearly a lie. He'd never have allowed it once she'd learnt his evil secrets.

"The master said the same to my mistress's family. They lived south of London, six days' journey from here. Never once did she return to see them, and never once did he permit them to visit Lady Roth here." From the ambry shelf, Mabel retrieved matching blue slippers and aided her in slipping them on her feet before carrying the wooden chair closer to the fire and patting the seat. "Come and sit. Your hair will dry quicker before the fire."

She sat and tapped her knees as Mabel picked up the brush, separated her hair into sections and gently combed. As her maid worked each section in soothing strokes, detangling the mess, her thoughts returned to Winterly, Avery, and Father. None of them would allow this kidnapping, and she didn't doubt they'd be descending on Rothgale before too long. Over her shoulder, she said to Mabel, "There is a difference between me, your late mistress, and Roth's first two wives. My family live directly next door at Hillhurst Hall."

A flicker of hope gleamed in Mabel's eyes. "Night is falling now as we speak. After I've tended to you, I could

THE EARL'S SECRET BRIDE

sneak out and run to the hall."

"You would take that risk for me?"

"Of course, my lady." A firm nod.

"I'll accept your offer, but only on one condition. You mustn't leave until Roth and Hobbs are no longer concerned with what is going on about the house, but instead are only concerned with me. I won't have your life placed in jeopardy."

"Understood." Mabel set the brush back on the dressing table and wrung out the sponge in the bathwater. From the top drawer of the dresser, she selected a strip of ribbon, tore a piece off the sponge and tied the ribbon around it, then she picked up a flask from the drawer and popped the cork. Mabel tipped liquid from the flask into the sponge, the scent of liquor wafting toward her.

"What is that?" she asked the lass.

"My mistress took precautions in order to stay off any possible pregnancy. A woman can use sponges or a plug of cloth to keep from getting with child, and she used one regularly since she didn't wish to carry a baby who would end up becoming a puppet at Roth's evil hands. Only once did she ever get with child during her five and a half year union with the master, or I should say with Hobbs since he was the one to lie with her."

"You're aware of Roth's impotence?"

"There was naught my lady didn't speak to me about. I kept her secrets, just as I'll keep yours." The maid passed her the flask. "This is brandy. You can use vinegar or lemon juice with the sponge, but brandy is easiest to keep in the drawer. Neither the master or Hobbs ever took any notice of it since my mistress enjoyed a tipple each night before bed."

"Thank you. I appreciate your aid." She handed the flask back.

"I'll tell you how to use this sponge." With the brandy-soaked sponge in hand, her maid knelt in front of her and murmured, "The sponge needs to be positioned high enough to ensure Hobbs doesn't feel it inside you, then the ribbon must be tucked away inside as well. You'll need to fish around to find the ribbon afterward but once you do, you'll be able to safely tug the sponge out. Is there anything else you need to know?"

"I'm so sorry I never got to know her." Her heart heaved for Mabel's late mistress and placing her full trust in the maid, she accepted the sponge and inserted it as far as it would go. Once done, she rinsed her hands in the bathwater and gave Mabel her most courageous smile.

Courage she would hold onto for this entire night. Come hell or high water, she would.

Chapter 14

With the floor plan memorized and the drawing of it tucked away into his pocket, Winterly braced himself as he and Avery stepped into Rosamonde's bedchamber after leaving Hillhurst and his wife downstairs in Hillhurst's study. He'd needed to see for himself the state of Rosamonde's room and if there were any further items that the maid hadn't found which might relate to the kidnapping. Clues as such. Certainly after the maid and butler had made a full check of the house, they'd found no further signs of Rosamonde. She had most certainly been taken, by way of the cellar tunnel by the looks.

Gritting his teeth, he touched the smear of blood streaked across Rosamonde's paneled wall and the rage which had been simmering away within him exploded into utter and complete fury. He would most certainly need his saber, pistol, and a few discreet blades strapped to his body when he left.

Beside him, Avery too spied the blood and cursed

Roth to hell.

He gripped Avery's shoulder after his friend had pummeled the wall. "We'll both send him to hell, although only after we've rescued Rosamonde and brought her safely home. She must be all we think about right now, and securing her rescue."

"Agreed." Avery rubbed his knuckles against his sides.

"We'll leave at dusk since we'll need the dark of the night on our side as we infiltrate the manor." Out Rosamonde's window, the gray day had turned even grayer throughout the afternoon, the threat of rain now ominously close. "Before we leave, I need to speak to my mama and sister and explain what's happened. Your mother will need a friend during the difficult hours ahead and my family would never disclose the truth to another. They will also offer any support the countess requires."

"I need to attend to a few issues myself. I'll meet you at the stables. Right on dusk."

"Will do." He left Avery and strode downstairs. Along the passageway, he came upon the butler walking toward him and he slowed and asked, "I'm looking for Lady Winterly and Lady Olivia."

"They're taking tea in the blue drawing room, my lord." The butler motioned toward the south wing.

"Thank you." He continued along the deep red and gold woven runner, passing a maid who dusted the frame of a landscape painting adorning the wall. He jerked to a halt before back-stepping to the painting which held the countess's signature in the bottom right corner. The maid bobbed her head and swept away with her duster, disappearing farther down the passageway. He'd passed this painting dozens of times over the years, admiring it on more than one occasion, but this time he couldn't help but be captured by the sheer beauty of the piece. The rippling waters of the lake glistened and in the center lay the island with its domed Grecian temple and heavily leaved trees with wide boughs rocking in the wind. A young girl knelt on the shoreline in pretty pink short skirts, a small pail in one hand as she collected pebbles, her golden locks blowing about her face from underneath her pink bonnet. The girl was the focus of the painting, no matter her tiny form on the beach before the temple. He could even make out the child's sweet cheeks and dimples either side of her smiling mouth. Her blue-green eyes reflected the color of the water and sheer happiness bubbled from her angelic face.

The soft tread of moving wheels broke his reverie and he turned to find the countess being pushed in her wheeled chair by a footman. She raised a hand to the footman as she drew up beside him, then dismissed the liveried servant with a flick of her fingers. Once the young man had disappeared around the far corner of the passageway, the countess said, "I hope you don't mind that I join you?"

"Not at all. You are extremely talented. This is Rosamonde, correct?"

"Yes, my daughter was eight years of age at the time when I painted this picture." Tears pooled in her eyes as she gazed at the painting. "My little Rosamonde. She would collect pebbles in that pail then try to skip them as her brothers did. It wasn't long though before she became more proficient than them. Even now, Avery, Kipp, West, and William can't skip stones like she can." She returned her watery gaze back to him as she reached one gloved hand for his.

He caught her hand and hunkered down to her eye level. They looked at each other for long seconds, both lost for a moment until finally, he forced himself to blink away his own watery tears. In a whisper, he murmured, "I have fallen in love with your daughter."

"Yes, your pain is as deep as her father's and mine. I can see the love you have for her shining in your eyes." A whisper in return. "My husband is currently scouring through the initial loan document between him and Roth, hoping to find something which might aid us. He is rather worried about Roth's coming wrath which will explode once we've found and brought Rosamonde home. Although my husband no longer wishes for you and Avery to leave for London, but for you and my daughter to speak vows as swiftly as possible. There will already be a scandal with what Roth has done, one we'll never be able to halt from spreading considering the damning nature of it. We'll worry about securing the funds afterward."

"Roth has a great deal to answer for." He patted his pocket which held the floorplan. "I have your detailing drawing and if she is at the manor, Avery and I will bring her home this very night." He rose to his feet, moved in behind her chair and pushed her toward the blue drawing room. "Your son and I shall ensure Roth suffers greatly for his actions, that he never attempts to take another innocent young lady into his home again. Our two families have now united in this cause, and we are a decidedly stubborn lot who won't rest until all is made right."

"I do like how you think, my lord."

"Please, call me Richard. We will be family as soon as I can manage it, and it seems only right that you address me by my first name."

"Thank you, Richard, and I insist you call me Elizabeth." She smiled at him over her shoulder as he steered her into the blue drawing room.

"I would be honored to do so, Elizabeth." In the spacious room, a marble-topped side table held a vase of yellow and white lilies and perfumed pink roses, while directly above it on the blue silk-papered walls hung an elegantly framed painting of the earl and the countess's children—four strong and honorable sons and one charming daughter. He smiled at Mama and Olivia as they sipped steaming tea and embroidered together, then he eased Elizabeth's chair next to where his family sat before brushing a kiss across Mama's cheek and then his sister's. There were no staff or servants about, so he proceeded to tell his family all that had happened. It took several minutes—all tense and difficult—to explain Rosamonde's abduction and their plan to secure her release.

"That's dreadfully awful." Mama clasped Elizabeth's hand. "I'm so sorry, my dear friend."

Olivia teared up and dabbed her wet cheeks with a handkerchief, her gaze on him. "Promise me, brother, that you'll find her."

"I promise." He wouldn't accept any other outcome. "Avery and I are about to ride out, our coming mission one of covert secrecy and great stealth."

"We'll pray for you." Olivia swamped him in a hug. "Be careful."

"We shall all weather this storm together." Now that

he'd assured himself that Rosamonde's mother was in good hands, he swiftly departed the room.

In his bedchamber, he removed his weapons from his valise, strapped his saber to his hip, tucked his pistol in the pocket of his breeches, and strapped on two daggers, one at his ankle and the other at his wrist. Swinging his heavy black cloak over his shoulders, he marched outside to the stables where Avery already awaited him. They requested the stable hands saddle their horses and as the skies turned from gray to the darkest midnight blue, they mounted and galloped across the fields and passed through the forest bordering the Hillhurst and Roth properties on Hillhurst's northernmost boundary.

A short distance from their destination, they dismounted and looped the reins of their mounts to a tree. With a coil of rope slung over one shoulder, he weaved through the tall pines between them and the manor, Avery following only a few steps behind him. Once he caught the scent of smoke on the breeze and candlelight flaring from the front windows of Roth's country estate, he slowed his pace and knelt behind a bush.

Avery hunkered down beside him.

Keeping his voice low, he murmured to Avery, "Roth might be arrogant but he isn't stupid. If Rosamonde is here then we should expect several guards to be on duty."

"Guards we need to dispatch before we enter the manor."

"Exactly. Let's take another look at your mother's drawing." Winterly slipped it from his inner jacket pocket and unfolded it. By the meager light of the moon, he turned it about until he'd positioned it so it matched the manor standing before them.

Avery tapped the rear of the manor where the countess had drawn the servants' entrance near the stables. "Let's circle the entire perimeter, disabling any guards we see along the way, then we'll sweep back around and enter via the servants' entrance."

"That's a sound plan." A long driveway to their right led directly up to the manor's circular front entrance where mounted statues stood either side of the steps leading to the impressively tall front doors. With three floors in total, the uppermost floor holding turrets at each corner of each wing, it appeared a monstrosity of a residence. A service wing was set a short distance from the main wings of the house, and he rose from his crouch and half bent over, made his move.

On silent feet, he and Avery crept between two rows of yellow and white flowering bushes, his hood over his head just as Avery's was. He halted at certain points, searching for any possible threat. A guard stood on duty in the shadows under one tree and he handed the rope to Avery, who snuck in behind the guard and caught the man in a choke hold, one hand over the guard's mouth to halt him from yelling a warning. The guardsman tried to tear Avery's hands away, but Avery tightened his hold on the man and he finally succumbed to the pressure on his windpipe and slumped in Avery's arms. The two of them bound the guard's hands and feet then tied him to a tree before gagging him in case he awoke.

Onward, they weaved through the garden, ensuring their coverage.

When they spotted a second guard, they disabled him

in the same manner. A third guard remained on duty outside the servants' entrance, so they left him for now and swept around the entire width of the manor a second time. They found another guard, put him out of action, then returned to the rear.

With his heart beating a ferocious tempo, he gestured for Avery to halt with him behind a bush. He pointed to the final guard who patrolled the servants' entrance, the man moving back and forth as he kept everything in his view. Leaning into Avery's ear, he whispered, "The sheer number of guards on duty signal to me that Rosamonde is indeed inside."

"I agree. My sister is in there." Avery growled low under his breath. "I want to gut Roth for what he's done."

"Then let's get inside and begin the gutting." His chest ached, his frustration burning fierce and hot as he scoured the darkened area outside before sliding his dagger from his ankle sheath. He palmed the hilt and bit out, "It's time to slay the enemy."

As the moon disappeared behind a thick, dark cloud, he snuck out from his hidden spot behind the bush and with a flick of his wrist, sent his blade flying, his aim for between the man's eyes. The guard grunted as his blade hit its mark. The guard's eyes rolled back and before the man could hit the ground, Winterly caught him and hauled him back to the bushes. He dumped the body in the scrub before nodding at Avery. "Time is of the essence."

They snuck inside with barely a creak of the door as they opened it.

Following the path laid out by the countess's drawing, they kept their hoods over their heads and followed the warren of passageways toward the front foyer where the staircase led upward to the first and second floors. They bounded up the stairs, came around the first corner and barreled into Roth's butler. The man opened his mouth to shout but Winterly slammed his fist into the butler's gut and Avery scooped a marble bust from a nearby column and slammed it over the man's head. The servant went down without even a whimper.

"We need to hide him," Avery hushed as he opened a side door and peered inside the darkened interior. "This is the game room by the looks, and it's clear."

"The game room sounds perfect to me." Clutching the butler's booted feet, he hauled the man into the room which housed the heads of game on every wall. Lifeless eyes stared back at him from every direction. He closed the door after himself and hurried after Avery down the hallway.

Up another flight of stairs, they rushed on soundless feet, then dashed through the gallery displaying portraits of the previous Marquesses of Roth. Under the light from a candle flickering in a wall sconce, he studied the drawing again to be sure of their next move. He had no desire to make a mistake now, not when they were so close to Roth's personal chambers. Without uttering a word to Avery, he tapped the spot where they now stood, then where they needed to be. Avery nodded his head and motioned for him to lead the way.

He tucked the drawing away, gripped the hilt of his saber strapped to his hip and hastened along the meagerly lit hallways. When he reached the final stretch, he spied another guard standing across from a closed door and he slowed and motioned for Avery to halt as well.

Avery didn't halt though—he bolted toward the guard with his dagger in hand and without any hesitation, buried it deep into the guard's gut, one hand slamming over the man's mouth to halt any cry for help. All but a light, muffled moan escaped the guard before his eyes flickered shut and he drooped in Avery's hold.

"Get the door," Avery demanded with a whisper as he back-stepped toward him.

Winterly opened the nearest door, thankfully to a small linen room, and motioned for Avery to drop the guard inside.

"Luck has been on our side this night." Avery stuffed the man underneath the lowest shelf holding piles of fresh linen.

"My bet is that Rosamonde is in there." He gestured to the chamber the man had been guarding.

"That would be my bet too." A nod from Avery.

"Then let's be away." Closing his eyes, he sent a quick prayer upward for Rosamonde before tipping his ear against the door of the chamber. Not a noise traveled to him from within. He snuck inside and halted at the sight of a maid kneeling on the floor next to a bed covered in a gray and black tartan blanket, her elbows pressed to the mattress.

She glanced at him, scars crisscrossing one side of her face, her pale eyes softening as hope bloomed within them, then she pressed a finger to her lips as she stood. She hurried across to him and Avery, tugged them both inside and closed the door. Leaning back against it, she murmured, "Are you here for my mistress?"

"Yes, I'm the Earl of Winterly and with me is Lady

Rosamonde's brother, Viscount Avery." He searched the maid's face. "What is your name?"

"Mabel, my lords." She bobbed into a curtsy.

"Where is she?" Winterly asked her. "Lady Rosamonde?"

"In his lordship's bedchamber." She motioned to a connecting door which remained closed. "There is a dressing room, then another door which opens directly into the lord's chamber. Hobbs is in there too."

"Who is Hobbs?"

"Lord Roth's half-brother, who is as violent as the master. Please take all care. They will be armed. Roth has a foil hidden within his cane."

"We're armed as well." He gripped the hilt of his saber. "It seems you don't mind our arrival?"

"Not one bit, my lord. It is a blessing you are here. My lady made me promise I couldn't leave the house to sneak out for Hillhurst Hall until she was ensconced within the lord's chamber."

"I take it you won't call any attention to our arrival then?"

"Certainly not." She pointed at the door. "Please hurry."

Yes, no more could they delay.

Chapter 15

"May I pour you a sherry, Lady Rosamonde?" Roth asked in a sugary tone which had the hairs on the back of Rosamonde's neck rising.

"No, I would prefer something far stronger." She remained standing with her hands clasped in front of her, the blue skirts of her day gown sweeping the white woolen mat before the fireplace.

"I have some Scottish whisky. Is that strong enough?" He poured a splash into three glasses, picked up the first and handed it to Hobbs who lazed in a blue padded chair with his booted feet extended toward the warmth of the fire, then he collected the remaining two glasses and extended one to her. "By the way, I do approve of your show of courage. Which means it'll make the moment when I break you all the more satisfying."

Not prepared to show him any trepidation, she accepted the glass and sent him a narrowed look over the rim as she sipped it. The strong brew burned its way down her throat. Living this close to the Scottish border and having a father who enjoyed a glass of whisky from time to time had allowed her to garner a taste for the strong brew too. She took a second sip, the golden-amber liquid not burning this time but instead sending a rush of warmth to her belly.

Roth collected his walking cane where he'd propped it against the drinks' table, then eased down onto the end of his bed. He puffed away on his pipe, smoke curling into the air.

This chamber had to have been the largest chamber she'd ever beheld, what with it being twice the size of her father's rooms. A chandelier hung from the high-beamed ceiling, the candles all alight, while a strange wooden rack with a high, sturdy beam across the top, held ropes hanging down from it.

"I see the torture rack has drawn your interest." Roth sipped his whisky.

"Pardon?" She gulped another mouthful and looked anywhere but at the rack.

"If you don't comply with my demands, then you'll be strung from that rack, naked, your arms and legs outstretched as you dangle, for days on end if need be."

Another mouthful and feeling a little light-headed, she set the glass down on the side table before gripping one edge of the mantel over the lit fireplace.

"Lift the hem of your gown, my lady." Smirking, Roth extended his legs out lazily. "Slowly. Very slowly."

"The lady will do no such damned thing!" Winterly appeared in the doorway of the dressing room, his saber in hand.

She swayed at the vision he made, such a beautiful vision, no matter the scowl darkening his face. Avery swept through after him and she bolted in their direction.

Hobbs caught her first, snatching her around her waist and hauling her back against him. With the cold steel of his dagger jabbing into her throat, blood trickled down the front of her gown. Big splotches of red splattered the floor.

A blade flew from Avery's hand and *thump*.

It landed above her head, directly inside Hobbs's open mouth, as if he'd swallowed the blade whole.

Avery caught her as Hobbs toppled backward, the dagger at her neck clattering on the floorboards in front of her. Avery whipped his neckcloth from around his neck and pressed it against her wound. "I'm so sorry, Rosamonde. How badly did he cut you?"

"Since I'm not lying on the floor as he is, I believe I shall survive." The cut throbbed as she snuck her fingers under Avery's and held the cloth in place. "I can look after myself. Go and help Winterly."

Roth had released his foil from his cane and charged Winterly.

Winterly swung his saber and caught Roth's blade dead center. Steel clanged loud against steel as the two of them fought hard and fast. Such a blur of movement. Winterly was on the defense, blocking each of Roth's strikes, then he changed the flow of the battle as he thrust one foot forward and pushed Roth backward. With one hefty blow after another, Winterly forced Roth to retreat and the marquess stumbled on the mat before the fireplace. Roth went down, his head hitting the hearth, the fire poker nestled in its stand stabbing through his back and spearing his chest. Blood gushed everywhere, his eyes rolling until the whites showed.

She gagged, dry-heaving as Avery tucked her head against his jacketed shoulder. "It's over," her brother murmured in her ear as he squeezed her tightly to him. "Neither of those men can ever harm you again."

"Let me see Rosamonde's wound." Winterly sheathed his blade, was at her side in a flash.

"Richard." She released her brother and clutched ahold of her hero. "I knew you'd come for me, both you and Avery. I had no doubt about it."

"Your cheek is bruised and your lip is split." A low growl rumbled from his chest. "I need to kill Roth."

"You already have." She grasped his face in her hands. "How did you get inside? There is a guard outside my door, and the butler will surely return. Roth asked him to bring up a tray."

"The butler is currently napping in the game room. I'm afraid there have been a few casualties tonight as Avery and I made our way to you." Gently tipping up her chin, he eased the cloth from around her neck wound. He inspected the cut with great care then called toward the connecting door, "Mabel, come."

Her maid appeared, her gaze going wide on the gory scene as she took in Hobbs's then Roth's prone bodies. Tears of clear relief pooled in her eyes and she sobbed with one hand clutched to her chest. "Oh my, we are finally free. I never believed this day would ever come."

"It has come, and you are most certainly free." Winterly beckoned Mabel to him. "Lady Rosamonde requires your care. She suffered a cut from Hobbs's dagger when he restrained her."

"Let me see it." With one stubby finger, Mabel touched her neck and inspected the wound. "Bring her to Lady Roth's chamber. My late mistress suffered injury after injury from her husband and her chamber is well equipped with medical supplies."

"Will do." Winterly kept one arm around her waist as he eyed Avery. "Take care of this mess."

"I'll do my best." Avery nodded at her. "Don't go finding any more trouble tonight."

"I won't." She allowed Winterly to steer her back to Lady Roth's chamber. He eased her down onto the end of the bed, then sat beside her.

Mabel foraged in the dresser drawer, tipped brandy onto a clean cloth and dabbed her wound. "It has ceased bleeding, which is a good sign."

"Does it require stitches?" Winterly asked as he rubbed her back since she'd winced from the sting of the brandy on her neck.

"I'd rather use a sticky tree sap on this wound rather than stitches. It holds restorative, healing qualities and seals a wound without leaving a scar. Does that suit you, my lady?" Mabel asked her.

"Yes, it suits me very well." She absolutely adored this young maid who she intended on keeping. Clasping Mabel's arm, she asked, "I have a request. Would you consider returning with me to Hillhurst Hall and being my new lady's maid? I currently share a maid with my mother, but I already don't know what I'd do without you. You must say yes."

"I would be honored, my lady, to accept such an

esteemed position." Mabel beamed.

"Ida and Bertha must come too." She faced Winterly. "I cannot possibly leave any innocent servants behind when we depart this place and Mabel has already told me about the young girls here in this house."

"Then they shall come with us." Her hero looked into her eyes, such need swirling within them. "Tell me you're all right."

"I'm a little battered and bruised, but now that you're here, I'm going to be just fine." She cupped his cheek and smiled. "I love you." She didn't care if the whole world heard her declaration, not when she couldn't withhold those words any longer. "You are my hero, twice over now, no thrice since I must also count Gretna Green."

Mabel, still smiling, softly sighed and then she got busy searching for the bottle of tree sap, her back to them as she gave them a moment of privacy, or as much privacy as could be afforded in this situation.

"I love you too, which I mentioned to your mother. She is aware of the depth of my feelings for you." Winterly leaned in and whispered in her ear, "I need to kiss you."

A few scuffling noises echoed from Roth's chamber, then Avery appeared and brushed his hands against his sides. He glanced at Winterly. "I've covered Roth's and Hobbs's bodies in blankets for now, although we'll need to bury them soon. There will be a stench otherwise."

"Is there a night watchman in the village who can oversee the burial?"

"No, and we're a long way from the Bow Street Magistrate's Office in London so they might confirm that Roth's death was necessary."

"Then we'll need to write down our statements, as well as take Mabel's statement of what she saw this night. We are dealing with the death of one of the peerage, which won't go unnoticed within our Society."

"Wait." She lifted one hand. "Major Brekensworth is visiting his sister in the village. We could request his presence. He could come and aid where needed, to give his statement as well."

"A superb idea." Avery nodded. "I'll collect the major and return with him, but only after we've returned you safely home, my dear sister."

"Mabel is coming with us, as well as two young maids who are innocent of all that's gone on in this house of horrors. Their names are Ida and Bertha." She held still as Mabel smeared sap across her wound.

"I'll find them, then attempt to restore some order downstairs with the remaining servants." Avery rested a fleeting hand on Mabel's shoulder. "Thank you for all you've done for my sister this night."

"You are welcome, my lord." More tears pooled in Mabel's eyes and flowed free as she smiled, her relief and happiness evident to see.

Avery left to find the girls, his saber strapped to his hip as he marched out the door.

Mabel wrapped a thin length of clean white cloth around her neck and secured it with a knot before crossing to the ambry and hunting within. She returned with a double-breasted white spencer and a fur muff.

Rosamonde stood, pushed her arms through the sleeves of the spencer and stuck her hands into the muff. She would be warm now for her return home. Winterly led the way downstairs, her in the middle and Mabel taking the rear.

Avery met them in the foyer after he'd gathered the girls from the kitchens, then he opened the front door and made sure all remained clear outside before motioning for them all to join him.

On the front step, Rosamonde breathed in the fresh night air, the silence stark and deafening.

"Do you hear that?" Winterly stepped in front of her as the drum of horses' hooves suddenly penetrated the night, along with the clatter of wheels. A carriage emerged from around the bend in the driveway, the lamp atop spreading a golden glow across the coachman seated atop and two further liveried footmen standing on the rear board, men who served her father, the coach holding her family's Hillhurst crest.

"It's Father." She grasped Winterly's arm.

The coach drew to a halt and her father bounded from the carriage, cast a stricken look at her face and stormed toward them, his hat on his head and his dark cloak swaying from his jacketed shoulders. "I couldn't remain at Hillhurst Hall a moment longer."

She rushed forward and Father enfolded her in his arms, his warmth surrounding her as she burrowed her head even deeper into his shoulder. "I'm fine."

"You don't look fine. Your cheek is badly bruised, your lip split, and your neck is bandaged."

"It'll all heal."

"I'm going to kill Roth for what he's done to you." Father sent Winterly and Avery a sharp look. "Where is the blackguard? Tell me now so I can strangle him."

"He's already dead," Winterly answered. "His body remains in his chamber, that of his half-brother as well. Both of them were as evil as each other and now thankfully gone from this world. There have been other casualties this night as well, guards we had to silence for fear of being discovered before we reached the south wing, although there are three maids with us who are all innocent of any wrongdoing."

"Then they will join Rosamonde in the carriage and return to Hillhurst Hall immediately. I will gladly offer the maids positions in my home." Father continued to hold her tightly to him, as if he didn't wish to relinquish her. "With all these deaths," he said to Winterly and her brother, "we'll need to take statements."

"Yes, our thoughts exactly." Winterly brushed a hand gently down her back. "Sir, Avery intends on riding to the village and requesting Major Brekensworth's aid in overseeing the burials and taking of our statements."

"Yes, yes, Brekensworth is visiting his sister, a fine fellow he is, and currently on leave from his regiment across the English Channel."

"I'll ensure the ladies arrive safely home before I collect Brekensworth." Avery urged her from her father's arms and settled her inside the carriage before beckoning the three maids forward. The ladies all sat huddled together on the bench seat across from her, while Avery stepped inside and sat at her side.

"I'll see you soon." Winterly blew her a discreet kiss as he closed the door.

The carriage jerked forward then the horses settled into a smooth gait as they traveled down the driveway. She pressed a hand to the window as Winterly, Father, and their two footmen strode inside the manor.

The trees shimmered a silvery-green under the moonlight as they bumped along the road back to Hillhurst Hall. Home. She would soon be home.

Not long later, they rattled up their long driveway from the main road, the front latticed windows all aglow with candlelight.

Once they'd pulled to a stop at the front door, Simmonds welcomed them home and Olivia engulfed her in her arms. Winterly's mother swept in and embraced her, tears flowing down her cheeks.

Mother awaited her in her wheeled chair and she stumbled toward her, dropped to her knees and got enveloped in her mother's wonderful and warm hold.

They all sobbed, her family's love surrounding her.

So much love.

She absorbed it all and held it tight in her heart.

Chapter 16

Hillhurst Hall was deathly quiet as Winterly entered through the front door with Hillhurst and Avery just as the dawn sun broke across the horizon in a blaze of golden-yellow. It was a new day, a new beginning to his life, for both him and his new bride. His secret bride. A bride he could no longer remain apart from, not when all he wished to do was stride upstairs and join her in her chamber. Right now, he needed to be wherever she was, and on that note he faced Hillhurst and Avery at the base of the stairwell as he prepared to offer them his full confession. "I have news, unexpected news."

"There could nothing more unexpected than what we've discovered this night at Rothgale Manor." Hillhurst slapped him on the shoulder. "But go right ahead, provided it is good news, I'll be happy to hear it."

He raked a hand through his dark hair. "I must apologize first, but when I feared leaving Rosamonde and traveling to London without her, I didn't want to take the risk of departing without first ensuring she had the safety of my name."

"What are you saying?" Avery frowned as he gripped the top of the newel post.

"That I'm already married to her."

That statement got wide eyes from both men.

"How?" Hillhurst asked first when he recovered from his clear shock.

"Before the kidnapping, I stole her away to Gretna Green and we spoke vows."

"You sly old fox." The earl suddenly chuckled with a beaming grin. "Congratulations on your marriage."

"You're not mad?"

"After Rosamonde went missing, I told my wife I no longer wished for you and Avery to leave for London, but for you and my daughter to speak vows as swiftly as possible. I'm exceedingly glad to hear you stole her away and wed her. That will help greatly in stemming any gossip which will surely arise from all that's happened."

"Sir, we hadn't initially intended on telling anyone, not when neither she or I had wished to cause a scandal. My intention was to wait until I'd secured the funds for the loan, handed them to you for repayment to Roth, then for her betrothal with the marquess to come to a natural end. I had hoped she would get the chance to enjoy a Season in town, that I might be able to court her properly before we announced an engagement. No one was supposed to learn of our secret marriage, but things have certainly now changed, just as you've said."

"There is also the fact that since I stole my own wife away to Gretna Green, I can hardly berate you for doing the same." The earl removed his cloak, folded it over one arm and extended his hand. "Young man, welcome to the family."

Shaking the earl's hand, gratefulness bloomed in his chest.

"Yes, welcome to the family." Avery slapped him on the back. "I can now call you my brother, as well as my best friend."

"You surely can." He faced his new father-in-law. "I need to see her now," he admitted. "Do I have your permission?"

"Of course you do. I'll inform my wife of the happy news of your marriage and tomorrow night, once we've all had a good day's rest, we'll celebrate your nuptials. There will be a feast to end all feasts."

"What of the loan to Roth?" He couldn't ignore the fact that it still existed.

"Seeing as Roth is now deceased, and that it might take some time to locate his closest male heir among his relatives, I no longer foresee any issue there. It was Roth alone who wished to break our loan agreement and demand an early repayment. Now, instead, I shall repay the loan to his estate once the remaining five years have expired." With a wave over his shoulder, Hillhurst whistled a merry tune as he continued on along the lower passageway toward his and his wife's bedchambers.

Avery winked at him, saying nary another word as he bounded up the stairway.

He was free of his secret. Free to take Rosamonde as his wife in every way. Free to ensure they spent the rest of their lives close to each other and near their families. He'd never tear her away from her loved ones, which was a promise he made right then and there in his heart to her. Breathing deep, he raced up the stairway, knocked on her chamber door and waited.

"Who is it?" A sleepy answer.

"Your husband."

He waited only two seconds before the door swung open and his bride stood there in her ivory nightgown, her bare toes peeking out from under the hem, and her golden hair falling in loose waves over her shoulders and down her back. Her beautiful blue-green eyes appeared wide as she looked in both directions down the passageway. "Someone might see you, or hear you."

"I've just informed your father and brother about our dash to Gretna Green. The earl then congratulated me on our marriage and stated that he could hardly berate either of us for what we did when he'd done the same with your mother. I also have his permission to be here, and not just outside your chamber, but inside it." Her cream and yellow floral drapes were pulled across her windows, although the early rising sunshine backlit the pale colors from the other side.

"Oh my." She fluttered a hand over her mouth. "Then please, do come in."

He closed the door after himself, locked it and began dispensing with his clothes. He kicked off his Hessian boots, shrugged out of his jacket, unknotted his black cravat, unbuttoned his blue silk waistcoat, and peeled his dark shirt over his head. As he stripped off his black breeches, he managed to walk his bride backward toward her yellow canopied bed covered in yellow and cream bedcovers. "Are you tired, my love?"

"I've only had an hour's sleep. I was too worried about you to catch much rest." The backs of her knees hit her mattress and she toppled back with a giggle.

"I've been worried about you too." He eased down on top of her, the thin cotton of her nightgown all that remained between them. Taking care, he lightly stroked one finger down her bandaged neck then kissed the spot where she'd been hurt and reveled in the moment as she softly sighed.

"Are you about to ravish me, my lord?"

"That all depends if you're willing to be ravished. It has surely been a difficult night for you." He didn't wish to push her beyond her limits, not after all she'd been through following her abduction.

"Yes, please, I would very much like to have my husband ravish me. Although there is something I haven't had the chance to tell you." Slowly, carefully, she unlaced the front laces of her nightgown and spread the linen. She exposed her breasts. Bruised breasts.

"Roth did this to you?"

"Yes, while I was out of it from the Belladonna, although I must have gotten my vengeance since I awoke from the sedative with blood underneath my fingernails from scratching the bald spot on his head. My breasts are sore, obviously."

"I'm sorry." She'd been mauled by a man he wished to bring back to life, just so he could kill him again. Slowly, he dipped his head and gently kissed around each mound until he'd smothered them in his love. Never would he allow another man to touch her again, to abuse her in such a way.

"Mmm, that's nice." She closed her eyes and stretched sinuously underneath him. "Your kisses are whisper-soft."

"Things are about to get much, much nicer." Tenderly brushing his lips across one corner of her lips, he made certain he didn't touch the split which had barely begun to heal.

"Stop teasing me and start showing me how very nice you can be."

He surely would.

He eased her arms from the sleeves of her nightgown then slid down her body to the end of the bed. "Lift up a little."

She did and he tugged her nightgown past her feet and tossed it onto the pile of his own clothing. He widened her legs, stroked along her inner thighs, his fingers gliding all the way to the crease of her groin. Head dipped, he nuzzled her mound covered in soft golden curls, spread her legs even wider and revealed all of her to his ravenous gaze. With a low rumble, he glided one finger along her slit. "I want my cock inside you, right here. I can't wait to join us together as one."

"Oh, please, yes. I want that too."

"Although we both need to wait a little longer first. I want to draw out your pleasure for as long as I can." He blew a breath across her folds and when she arched her back, he swept his tongue across her intimate flesh. Her decadent taste danced on his tongue and hell, he wasn't going to last long at all. Pushing two fingers deep inside her, he sucked her nub and laved her with attention.

"Richard, I'm going to come." She tunneled her

fingers through his hair and held onto him, pushing his head firmer against her.

"I know what you need." He speared his tongue deeper inside her channel, surging over and over again, right where his cock would soon be surging, and as she shuddered, her legs trembling and her core spasming, he rose up over top of her, pressed the head of his shaft against her entrance and plunged deep inside her.

With his hands planted either side of her head, he nuzzled her neck as her inner muscles clenched and dragged him in even deeper. He came apart, unable to hold on, his seed spurting from him in one hot pulse after another. No withdrawal method this time. He wanted to see her belly rounded with his child, for them to have a family of their own.

"You're my wife, always mine." Never had he felt so wonderfully complete.

This woman was his to love and protect for the rest of his life.

She was his secret bride, his to hold, always and forever.

Chapter 17

Sprawled nude across Winterly's chest within her yellow canopied bed, the warmth from her crackling fire washed over her. Never had Rosamonde known that a love like this could be hers. They'd slept for half the day after they'd made love earlier this morning, then joined together again when they'd both awoken hungry with a fierce need to touch each other. Now, she played her fingers through her husband's silky chestnut brown hair, his muscled body rippling with strength underneath hers. "I believe we need a honeymoon."

"I'm absolutely certain we do." He caught her hand and threaded their fingers together. "Will you come away with me for two weeks to my country estate? We can return to see your family fairly quickly if you need to, but I also need a little time alone with you, desperately."

"For some reason I thought my mother would struggle without me being here, but she also has my father and they are so in love and always have been. She will be fine without me for two weeks, or for however long we wish to be away for whenever we travel to London."

"Which reminds me. Your mother actually said something about that. She believed it was time for her to return to Society, to set her injury aside and live her life again. She doesn't wish to be the one to hold you back."

"She truly said that?"

"Yes."

"Oh my, how wonderful." She wriggled up, slung one leg over his hips and straddled him, her love for him filling and overflowing her heart. "Richard, secrets can be quite titillating, don't you think?"

"If you're meaning our secret marriage, then yes, exceedingly so." He wriggled underneath her, his cock jabbing into her bottom. "Kiss me, Rosamonde."

"Where would you like that kiss?" Staring him straight in the eyes, she scuttled back, wrapped one hand around the length of his cock and gave it a squeeze. "Since you enjoyed giving me so much attention below earlier this morning, then it must surely be possible for me to do the same with you?"

"Hell, yes." He shuddered in her hand, his breath whistling out and his cock getting harder and longer.

"Tell me what to do." Another squeeze.

"You're doing just fine on your own, without any instruction." He grazed his knuckles along her belly then swept lower and rubbed her nub.

"Then I shall follow my instincts." She dipped her head and tentatively licked the head of his cock. When he shuddered and moaned, she worked him in long pulls as she suckled him.

"Rosamonde, that feels so good." He rubbed her nub in a slow circle and she too shuddered.

No, she wanted to keep indulging herself in him. She clamped her mouth around him tighter and he hissed out another breath.

"Take care with your sore lip."

"My lip is healing rather swiftly."

"No more then, or else I'm going to come inside your pretty mouth." He gripped her backside, lifted her up and swept her underneath him as he rolled over top of her. With one powerful stroke, he thrust deep, their bodies completely entwined as one, their legs and arms tangled as he made breathless love to her. "I can't wait to live my life with you," he whispered against her lips.

"Richard, I want to raise a family with you." She gasped at the rightness of their union. "My mother would dearly love grandchildren."

"I haven't used the withdrawal method this day, not when I want you carrying my child, as soon as I can possibly manage it." Cupping the back of her head, he drew her mouth gently to his and kissed her so sweetly, so carefully, her pleasure always at the forefront of his mind.

This was where she belonged, with the man who had saved her as a young girl, and with the man who'd returned to save her twice more since. It was time to explore a new future with him.

The Earl of Winterly was her hero, would always be her hero.

Her life was about to get deliciously titillating.

The Prince's Bride

~ COMING NEXT ~

Regency Brides Series, Book Five

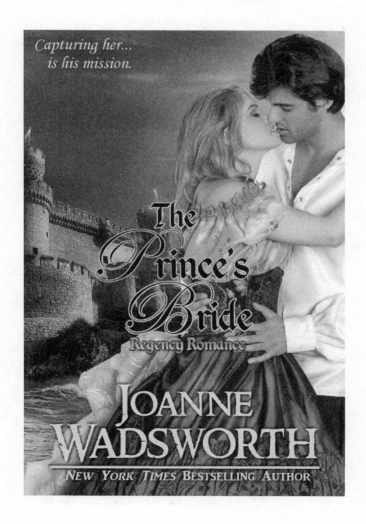

JOANNE WADSWORTH

Regency Brides

The Duke's Bride, Book One
The Earl's Bride, Book Two
The Wartime Bride, Book Three
The Earl's Secret Bride, Book Four
The Prince's Bride, Book Five
Her Pirate Prince, Book Six
Chased by the Corsair, Book Seven

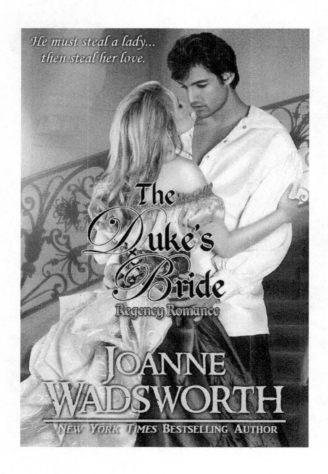

The Matheson Brothers

Highlander's Desire, Book One
Highlander's Passion, Book Two
Highlander's Seduction, Book Three

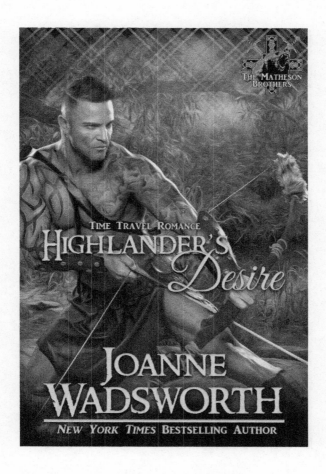

The Matheson Brothers Continued

Highlander's Kiss, Book Four
Highlander's Heart, Book Five
Highlander's Sword, Book Six

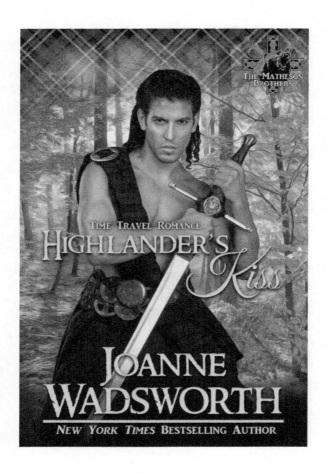

The Matheson Brothers Continued

Highlander's Bride, Book Seven
Highlander's Caress, Book Eight
Highlander's Touch, Book Nine

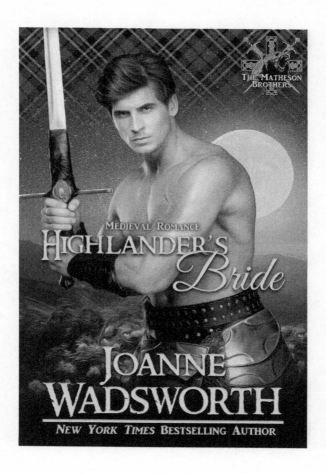

JOANNE WADSWORTH

The Matheson Brothers Continued

Highlander's Shifter, Book Ten
Highlander's Claim, Book Eleven
Highlander's Courage, Book Twelve
Highlander's Mermaid, Book Thirteen

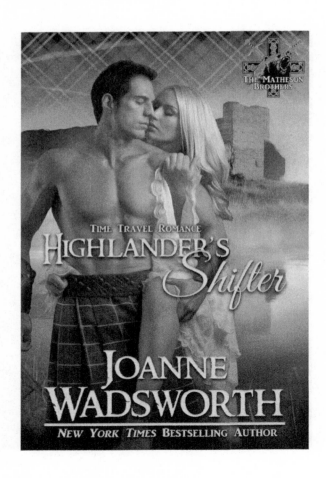

THE EARL'S SECRET BRIDE

Highlander Heat

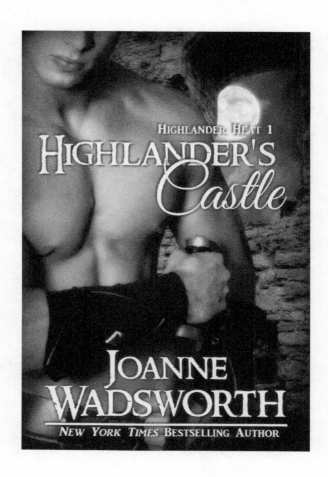

JOANNE WADSWORTH

Princesses of Myth

Billionaire Bodyguards

Billionaire Bodyguard Attraction, Book One
Billionaire Bodyguard Boss, Book Two
Billionaire Bodyguard Fling, Book Three

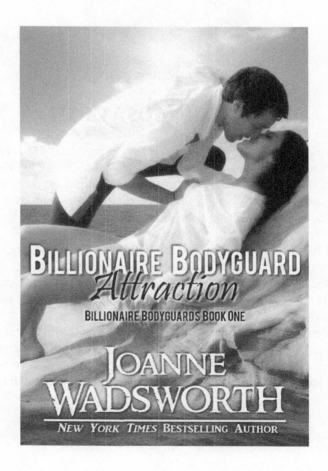

JOANNE WADSWORTH

Joanne Wadsworth is a *New York Times* and *USA Today* Bestselling Author who adores getting lost in the world of romance, no matter what era in time that might be. Hot alpha Highlanders hound her, demanding their stories are told and she's devoted to ensuring they meet their match, whether that be with a feisty lass from the present or far in the past.

Living on a tiny island at the bottom of the world, she calls New Zealand home. Big-dreamer, hoarder of chocolate, and addicted to juicy watermelons since the age of five, she chases after her four energetic children and has her own hunky hubby on the side.

So come and join in all the fun, because this kiwi girl promises to give you her "Hot-Highlander" oath, to bring you a heart-pounding, sexy adventure from the moment you turn the first page. This is where romance meets fantasy and adventure...

To learn more about Joanne and her works, visit
http://www.joannewadsworth.com

Made in the USA
Las Vegas, NV
15 February 2022

43987724R00121